HOLLOW BRIDGE PUBLISHING

RUNAWAY SOUL

TIFFANI QUARLES-SANDERS

RUNAWAY SOUL

Hollow Bridge Publishing
Montgomery, AL 36108

Copyright © 2017 by Tiffani Quarles-Sanders
ISBN 978-0-9863319-6-1 (Paperback edition)
ISBN 978-0-9863319-7-8 (Digital edition)

Cover by Julie Anne Ines
Editorial services provided by Erika's Editing
Proofreading services provided by PAWS Proofing Portal

PUBLISHER'S NOTE

CHAPTER 1

A hush blanketed the school as anticipation electrified the air. Jackie smiled. She didn't need to check the clock to know why every student was squirming with bubbling joy. It was time for dismissal.

"I've got my walkie," Jackie said to her secretary as she strode out of the office and into the hall. "If Ms. Edwards calls me back about the education plan, forward her to my cell."

"Will do," replied her secretary. The kids called her *Humpty Humphries*, but not in an unkind way. Ms. Humphries, an older woman, tried to do her job well, but she struggled a bit with technology. "I just got to remember how," she added.

Liberation was in the air. This was the one time of the day when students and staff alike had an almost-cosmic connection—all were determined to see the school day finished. The worst thing that could happen to a student was to get into trouble right before the last bell rang and have to stay after class. Likewise, most teachers sent out a special prayer into the universe in the hope that their students would *just act right* during this last hour of the school day. Having to keep a student after class meant that a teacher probably wouldn't make it home before sundown.

Jackie went outside and took her usual place in the field beside the main school building. The spot was slightly inclined, like a pitcher's mound. It gave her a good vantage point for watching over her students as they were dismissed. She surveyed the area.

To Jackie's left, cars were triple-parked. These were the parents of the younger kids, the kindergarteners through second-graders; they were always the most eager to get their children home. To her right, the less-enthusiastic parents of the older students had pulled their cars into a line.

Directly in front of her, busses hummed and hissed; drivers opened their doors for the impending onslaught. One gold-toothed, nest-headed driver waved over to her. "Hey, Ms. Macon," he yelled before licking his lips and grinning like a Cheshire cat.

Jackie waved at him and kept her distance. "Tell your wife I said hello, Randy," she called over the hum of the engines. His youngest son, a special needs student, had been one of her first students years ago—Randy's eyes had been roaming over to her ever since.

In response, the smile that had lifted the entirety of Randy's face fell quickly. He averted his eyes and focused again on the bus.

Jackie couldn't wait until the last day of the year, the day when she'd finally retire. She already knew how she was going to say good-bye to Randy. She was going to smile back at him, stomp up the steps of his bus, then slap those X-ray eyes right out of his face. She smirked, thinking of her full wrath unleashed. Ms. Jacqueline Macon, principal of the school, didn't go around slapping people. But Jackie Macon, the woman, couldn't stand married men who dogged around, or men who intruded into a woman's personal space, uninvited. Once her tenure was over, Jackie would be free to curse out any and all male whores who took advantage of their kind, sweet wives—she'd no longer have to worry about decorum or her reputation as an administrator. Yep, that was the truth of it; she was going to smack Randy silly.

Jackie took a deep breath, "Ten, nine, eight ..." she counted backwards to regain her cool—she needed a clear head to deal with the chaos of dismissal. Dismissal was an event at her school, and she took it seriously. There were three faculty assigned to patrol the front and side perimeters, with two other teachers assigned to secure the south side of the building. Once the bell rang, there would be no trampling, no misplaced students, and no unwanted guests. She made sure that her students were safe. As far as Jackie was concerned, her school was a safe haven amid the chaos of Los Angeles.

A male voice crackled through the walkie-talkie that was attached to her hip. "Ready. In place," came the signal. She looked toward the front of the building, where Mr. Andrews, her portly assistant principal, now moved into his position as well. His voice crackled over the walkie-talkie, "Ready. In place." Jackie looked toward the back of the building, where Coach Rick had taken up his usual *hero pose* in the open field. He placed his whistle to his lips.

"Thank you, guys," Jackie said into the walkie-talkie. "Ring the bell for release."

Jackie always ordered the school bell to be rang manually. There was an auto-timer option, of course, but Jackie always needed to verify with her own eyes that the area was safe and clear of danger before she let her students loose. They were her responsibility.

The bell sounded. The relative stillness was shattered as students buzzing with conversation and activity streamed outside.

Jackie waved, hugged, and scolded as needed. She could say, "Walk, don't run," in the same easy tone as, "I can't wait to see you tomorrow." An important quality for a principal. It made her popular among her students.

"Ms. Maaaccc!" a child drawled as she ran through the field. The name that reached Jackie's ears didn't sound anything like the name Macon, but that didn't matter to Jackie. The sound was still sweet all the same, and Jackie instantly knew to whom the small voice belonged. Only one student ever called her that.

The little girl had captivating eyes. Wide rounded eyes that narrowed at the outer ends and turned upwards. Huge, sideways-teardrop eyes that took up the bulk of the small girl's flat face. They contrasted strikingly against her sunshine-yellow dress.

"*You can tell the history of a person by the pits of their eyes. The soul speaks from there.*" Jackie heard her mother's voice in her mind more and more often these days. Perhaps it was a sign of aging: things that she had wished time had erased were coming back to her all the more frequently.

"Ana! Are you good, or are you good-good?" Jackie

asked the tiny brown girl who had now locked her arms around Jackie's knees.

"Good-good." Ana bounced with a smile. The teacher's aide who sauntered up behind Ana huffed.

"You sure do have a lot of energy today," Jackie said. Ana bounced some more in reply.

"I was walking her to her bus, but she had to come over and see you," the aide explained.

"Ms. Mac is so nice," Ana said as she looked up at Jackie. "She takes care of us."

Once again, Jackie was taken aback by the child's eyes. She beamed down at the sweet girl. Jackie's gut swirled, and she swallowed back a thick, familiar swelling of emotion. She genuinely cared for all of her students, and she made sure she nurtured each and every one of them in some way, but Ana was special. Ana needed her.

Jackie was almost sure Ana had some type of learning disability, and she'd finally convinced the girl's parents to have their daughter evaluated—the tests were scheduled for next week. Jackie was grateful that she'd identified the issue while Ana was still in kindergarten—early detection was key. Once the results came back, Jackie would make damn sure Ana got the available public-school service she needed.

"It's time to leave," the aide told the child, apparently unmoved by Jackie's special connection to Ana. "Ms. Macon, Ana was just determined to see you."

Static buzzed on Jackie's walkie-talkie, then Ms. Humphries's voice came to life. "Don't forget the principals' district meeting at four o'clock." Jackie sighed. Another wasteful meeting, another unnecessary drive through L.A. traffic. She wouldn't miss that part of her job.

"Bye-bye. See you tomorrow, Ana," said Jackie, smiling.

Ana clapped joyfully at the idea of seeing *Ms. Mac* again the next day.

✄

The district principals' meeting was already underway when Jackie slipped in fifteen minutes late. Jim, who was in the middle of a presentation, frowned at her before he clicked to his next slide.

Jim continued his presentation. "We are about to make our children safer. The new law passed earlier this month, and the state is requiring immediate enforcement without delay."

"What new law?" Jackie thought to herself. She thought for a moment that it might be related to the state's new testing guidelines until Jim revealed his next slide:

AS OF MARCH 31, 2012, FINGERPRINTING AND BACKGROUND CHECKS WILL BE MANDATED FOR ALL CALIFORNIA PUBLIC AND PRIVATE TEACHERS, ADMINISTRATORS, STAFF, BUS DRIVERS, AND CHILDCARE WORKERS.

"We're going to set up three stations throughout the district and get the job done in thirty days," Jim continued. "This is a real milestone for California. Parents and community leaders will be thrilled. And so should we all!"

Jackie's stomach tied itself into a knot. The audience around her was now clapping; she had to *will* herself to do the same. Her colleague Jane, seeing the alarmed expression on Jackie's usually stoic face, leaned over and asked, "Are you ok?"

Jackie nodded and continued to clap. She had heard something about new security measures a year ago, but she didn't recall any mention of fingerprinting. This could be a problem.

A hand in the audience went up. "Can you tell us how the system works?"

"It's pretty simple," began Jim, drawing his eyebrows together. "Names and fingerprints will be run through a nationwide database, and police will be alerted if any matches to known criminals are made. Now let's move on to the district Language and Math Skills Testing Report …."

Jackie tried to calm herself. Once she could think clearly, she would know what to do. It was a skill of hers, an instinct she had relied on since she was a young woman—it had never deserted her. She breathed in deeply. "Ten, nine, eight, seven …."

Her first thought was Peter. Was it time to tell him who, exactly, he had really married? Was it better if the news came from her? Was a private betrayal better than a public reckoning?

Could she run again? To where? She was now sixty-seven years old; she'd lived this life, this identity, for nearly fifty years. Until this moment her career—a proud and fulfilling career—was about to come to its natural end in less than three months' time. She and Peter were counting on her pension, but it was more than the money. Running again would mean giving up her legacy as a teacher, the only thing she was proud of, the only thing that had made her life count. She wasn't about to give that up.

The past swelled up inside her and long-buried memories washed through her mind. Richard, her first love. Richard, who she'd left behind when she was seventeen, although not by choice. She had been forced to close the door on their future, and once that door had been slammed shut, it could never be re-opened. In the decades since, the door had become a wall, then the wall itself had faded into a distant memory, just like all the other memories that had all but disappeared over time. Memories that, as the years passed, had come to belong to someone else, someone she almost no longer knew.

CHAPTER 2

J ackie slammed the car door. The anger coursing
through her was more intense than any she'd felt
in decades.

Her marriage had been mostly calm and even over
the years. Too weathered by life to ignite unnecessary
friction, both she and Peter preferred to keep things
smooth. If either she or her husband had an issue, they
simply found their separate spaces until things resolved
on their own. But tonight, Jackie's anger, fueled by fear,
had exploded out of her uncontrollably.

As soon as Jackie had arrived home from the district
principals' meeting, Peter had pounced on her with
excitement. He'd been offered a last-minute invitation to
a dinner party and he needed Jackie to accompany him.
Jackie well knew that Peter had spent the last year trying
to expand his business in advance of her retirement,
but she also knew a dinner party packed with potential
clients was the last thing she wanted to deal with
tonight—not with the hundreds of thoughts swirling in
her mind. Even still, she had changed quickly, slapped on
some lipstick, and pasted on her loving, docile-wife face.

That mask was what manufacturing types expected from the wife of a small hauling company owner; she had to put on a performance every now and again. Usually, she could play that game convincingly enough, but tonight… tonight had not gone well.

"I don't understand you," Peter snapped as he followed her into the living room. "Why are you acting this way? In twenty-five years of marriage, I've never seen you like you were tonight!"

Jackie turned on her heel and faced her husband. She wanted to push Peter, poke him—

maybe even punch him a little, just so that he could feel her frustration.

"That nosey bastard better be glad all I did was throw my drink in his face!" she hissed. She usually kept a tight rein on her emotions, but now she let her words cut through the air.

"He was just trying … to get to know you … to get to know *us*," Peter explained slowly, as if Jackie was hard of understanding.

Jackie retorted with a hand on her hip. "That man was interrogating me. You of all people know I won't ever let a man disrespect me. Business or not."

"He asked where you came from. It's polite conversation. You can hardly call that an interrogation." Peter swiped his large hand through the air as if he was erasing her objections. "You know I want to expand my fleet. There are solid opportunities in Texas! I'm trying to get the man's business."

"Well *I'm* not any of his business!" Jackie spat. "I only went to that damn dinner as a favor to you. That guy was being a pompous ass." Jackie took off her heels as she spoke. For an instant she thought she might throw one at Peter, but instead she held fast to her pump and used it to punctuate her next words. "All he wanted was to figure out what side of the tracks I grew up on! My maiden name and my kin have nothing to do with the competency of your business. I am not one to play with."

"That may be true, but people still go with who they know, even in the twenty-first century," Peter replied. "Small business owners want to know 'who you are' and 'what you're about' before they trust you with their livelihood. Andrew Druid is no different. You had no right to behave like that!"

"And he had no right to ridicule me," Jackie retorted. "I don't owe him an explanation of who I am. In fact, I don't have to tell that man a damn thing about my life."

As far as anyone in her very-carefully-crafted life knew, Jackie was from Denton, Texas, a college town. When this detail came up at the party, Andrew had immediately started rattling off street names and groups of people that she didn't recognize. In fifty years, Jackie had never once run into anyone from Denton, yet Andrew hailed from a town in the next county. She had tried to make it politely clear that she didn't want to talk about her *home*, but no matter how hard she tried to bring the conversation back to Peter and his small fleet of trucks, Andrew kept blathering on about his hometown. When he had laughed at Jackie for never having gone to the state fair, she was utterly undone. Her white wine hit Andrew's face before Jackie realized that her hand had even moved.

"I give up," Peter sighed. He pinched the bridge of his nose and inhaled.

"Peter," she said slowly, softening her tone. She didn't want to fight with him anymore. She hated fighting with him, hated straining the bond they shared. The woman Peter knew as his wife was the woman Jackie had become; most days she felt as natural in her identity—and with her husband—as any other woman.

Jackie hesitated a moment to keep her tears from welling up. The twelfth round bell had rung; it was time to return to their own corners. Wipe the wounds clean and figure out if anything was broken. Jackie turned toward the stairs; they both needed their space now, as was their habit.

She was halfway up the steps when she heard her husband's voice, now full, rich, and booming, force its way through the quieted, empty air.

"Tell me."

Jackie stopped in her tracks but didn't turn around. She wasn't sure she'd ever heard Peter use that tone of voice every before: it commanded an answer. Behind her, she could feel her husband waiting, filled with a patience that only comes from certainty. She was cornered.

"Tell you what?" Jackie replied, still without turning around. She had learned never to give a specific answer to an unspecific question, no matter the situation. Part of her held out hope that this wasn't the moment she'd been dreading for decades.

"Tell me why we never talk about your family," said Peter, taking a step closer. "Tell me why you've never been to a class reunion, why you've never had even one single relative call you. Tell me why you keep shutting yourself off from me."

Jackie felt herself waver. Maybe now *was* the right time. After this afternoon's events, she was going to need his support.

She turned and began walking back down the staircase, step-by-step. "Am I here every day with you?" she asked. "Do I come home every night?" She was now so close to Peter that she could count the pores on his face. "That's all you need to be concerned with. I don't have to explain myself to you... or to any other man."

"You think you're the only one with pain?" Peter shot back. "Jackie, you know everything about me from birth 'til today. You know what my life has been."

"The past doesn't matter," she said, wishing so hard that it was true.

Peter took a step back. He panned Jackie from head to toe before his gaze came to rest on her eyes. There was genuine concern and confusion in Peter's gaze although he looked at her as though a new person was standing in front of him.

"Then what are you holding onto so tight?" Peter dropped his words into the middle of the room; they fell on Jackie's heart with a palpable thud. Something inside her shattered—shards of glass began slicing her very soul.

"The past is... what it was." Each word Jackie expelled was hurt; her evasion slid across her tongue sourly. For an instant, though, she imagined that she could split the heaviness of her past in two and let Peter bear some of her burdens.

Peter took Jackie's hands. His wide calloused thumb smoothed over her creased knuckles. "Tell me what's haunting you," he pleaded. His voice was soft now, earnest. The booming had melted away.

Jackie calmed some at Peter's touch. He had been gentle with her, always. That was one of the things she loved about him. In her core, Jackie knew her husband only wanted what was best for her and their future.

"Let sleeping dogs lie," she said. The words came out like an apology. In fact, her words *were* an apology—she was truly sorry that she had hurt him.

Peter dropped her hands suddenly. His tone shifted into a firmness she knew she couldn't fight. "If you can't tell me about your past, I don't see how we can have a future. I've never pressed you on this Jackie, not even once… that's not our way. But after tonight, something's got to change."

His words stung badly and yet another rush of hurt coursed through her. Something in Jackie's face must've told Peter how desperately she wanted to share every memory and every moment that she'd kept so desperately hidden. But when she tried, all that came were tears.

❦

Alone in her study, Jackie unlocked the bottom drawer of her desk and took out her well-hidden lockbox. How many years had it been since she had allowed herself to look inside?

With a second tiny key, she unlocked the box, then

slowly lifted its gray metal top. The faded photo inside was wrapped in tissue paper, and the little half-finished knitted cap rested safely in its drawstring bag. The only mementos she had of the world she'd fled so long ago.

CHAPTER 3

J ackie stood at her desk and stared at the smartphone in her hand. Her usual morning routine—which she had abandoned today—was to do a quick email check, listen to her messages, consult her schedule for the day, then carefully consider the priority items on her to-do list. Instead, she was now staring at her cell phone and hoping to hear the special ring—an airy classic musical phrase that reminded her of her classic man—that identified her husband's calls. Her classic man, who hadn't come home last night for the first time in their marriage.

She had been so close to unburdening herself last night. When Peter had gone out for a walk, as he often did after their arguments, she knew the time was at hand. Jackie was never going to be ready to reveal her secrets, but she knew it had to be done. Peter deserved the truth and she needed him to know. Hopefully, all that came after that, they would navigate together.

But Peter never came home. After an hour or so, Jackie had checked the driveway; the car was gone. Hour after hour she waited. She hadn't even tried to sleep, she just sat and waited like Job for the Lord, like a mother for her lost child, like a lover for a smile. Anxiety had heightened her senses, putting them on high alert: every random engine and every car door closing had caught her attention.

Jackie had learned three things last night: her affluent neighbors had suspicious after-hours habits; her hearing hadn't diminished much with age; and, most importantly, that she'd finally lost her superpower of locking down on emotional bullshit. There wasn't even anyone she could call for comfort. She had never allowed herself close friendships; it wasn't safe.

She typed yet another text into her phone: "I'm sorry. I love you." It joined the growing list of one-sided messages on her screen. Her texts covered a range of emotions: "How dare you...!" to "Where are you?" to "Please come home," to "I can't do this without you," to "I shouldn't have yelled at you." This was really bad— Peter never ignored her texts; she'd never once had to wait more than fifteen minutes for a reply.

The sound of the morning bell snapped Jackie out of her misery. She was forced to set aside her weary and woe, and she was grateful for the distraction. She walked over to the full-length mirror hanging on the back of her door. She smoothed down her silk shirt, checked her designer shoes for scuffs, and then forced her face into a smile. She would be fine—and even if she wasn't, Jackie would make damn sure she looked the part.

The craziness kicked off as soon as Jackie took the first step out of her office. "I was just about to knock on your door," Ms. Humphries said. But before the secretary could speak another word, Jackie's walkie-talkie crackled to life.

"I need you in the kindergarten wing. There's a *knee* situation," the voice cried. Jackie took a deep breath. She had instructed her hall captains to never discuss a problem over the walkie. Instead, her monitors used code words to indicate what level of support they needed: *Toe* meant something minor; *ankle* meant an insight or question, nothing pressing; *calf* was a multi-layer issue with some urgency; *knee* was an emergency. As an administrator, Jackie gave her staff all the support she could, but—more personally—she thought of the codes as descriptors for how much shit she would be in if she didn't address the problem.

Luckily, there been relatively few knee situations during her tenure. Jackie was a natural problem solver. She could clamp down on an issue and set things right before the superintendent had to step in or lawyers needed be called. Jackie could fix just about anything for anyone, except when it came to her own problems.

"On my way," Jackie answered over the walkie. Like a woman on a mission, she strode into the hallway and powered through the morning swarm of teachers and students. Ms. Humphries followed on her heels.

"The superintendent's assistant called. He needs our fingerprinting schedule by Friday. He reminds you that no staff are exempt." Jackie stopped in her tracks, which caused Ms. Humphries to run into her boss's back, nearly knocking her over. "So sorry, Ms. Macon."

"Fine," Jackie snapped. "Put the schedule together—

No, wait, I'll tend to it later. Let me deal with whatever this is first." Ms. Humphries nodded, took the cue, and then scurried away.

Unexpectedly overwhelmed by the mention of fingerprinting, Jackie wasn't sure she could deal with a *knee* situation right now. She wanted to retreat into her office, calm herself, make a plan, and figure out how she was going to avoid having her fingerprints taken. Thirty days. That's what Jim had said at last night's meeting. She only had thirty days.

When she arrived on the scene, Jackie immediately found herself refereeing a custody agreement. A father had aggressively confronted a mother and her new husband for neglecting to drop off their daughter the previous weekend—which the father claimed was a violation of their custody agreement. Thankfully, a first-grade teacher had noticed the escalating tempers and had ushered all nearby students into a classroom. In the ninety seconds it had taken Jackie to arrive, things had turned truly ugly. Jackie issued a lock-down alert and called the police from her cell phone, just as the first punch was thrown.

The last thing that Jackie wanted to do was call the police, but by law she wasn't supposed to get physically involved in any confrontation unless a child's safety was immediately at risk. There was little more she could do other than shout at the men and beg them to come to their senses. Utter chaos—and the school day had barely begun.

Less than three minutes later, four male officers in two cars arrived to separate the brawling men. With police intervention, as well as with Jackie's staunch reminders that violence in a school zone carried extra penalties, the two men settled down fairly quickly. Everyone left of their own free will, with promises to handle their dispute in court.

After all three parents had left campus, Jackie turned to one of the policemen. "Thank you, officer, for your help," she said.

"Anything for you, Ms. Macon." The fresh-faced officer smiled. He placed a hand on his police belt, not too far from his gun; the action made Jackie's heart rate speed up a little. Gulping back the fear that had suddenly knotted in her throat, Jackie knew she needed to get the officer off campus as fast as she could. She plastered on a smile.

"Everything looks to be in order now," Jackie said as she took a step back. Interacting with the police had never bothered her before; sometimes officers were required as security at large-scale events on campus, and during the few times she had needed to call them in an emergency, she'd never given a second thought to the identity she was hiding. But now, with the staff fingerprinting looming over her, with the lie she'd been telling Peter all these years now sitting like a stone in her stomach, this officer—baby-faced as he was—was terrifying.

"You know, I've heard nothing but good things about this school since you've been principal," the officer said as he nodded and moved toward her. "When I was growing up, no one wanted to send their kids here, but you've really turned things around."

"I appreciate that, officer," replied Jackie. She took

a small, but involuntary, step backward. She hoped he hadn't noticed. To cover herself, she squinted at his badge. "Officer Bard. Thank you again."

Officer Bard reached forward and shook Jackie's hand. "We're here when you need us," he said as he walked away.

Jackie exhaled silently.

✄

Enjoying a moment of peace, Jackie walked slowly through the school's now-empty halls on her way back to her office. Just as her adrenaline rush began to subside, her cell rang—the airy, classic ring for which she had been waiting. Even though there was no one nearby, she stepped into an alcove before answering.

"Jackie, we need to talk."

CHAPTER 4

On her way into her office, Jackie stopped at Ms. Humphries's desk. "I'm leaving early today, around 2:00 p.m.; let Mr. Andrews know." She took a step forward, then back again. As offhandedly as she could, she asked, "Oh, and can you put the list on my desk for the superintendent? I'll review it in the morning."

Not wanting to aggravate her boss again, Ms. Humphries asked quietly, "The fingerprinting schedule, you mean?"

"That's the one," replied Jackie as she stepped into her office. She then spent the next hour going through her email and answering a few routine calls. Her focus and concentration had returned. Just knowing that Peter was willing talk had relaxed her shoulders by a full inch. Her lungs had now expanded back to their usual capacity; she could breathe properly again.

The intercom on her desk suddenly buzzed. "Ms. Macon," came Ms. Humphries' voice, "Sam is here to see you. He says it's important."

Jackie leaned toward the speaker, annoyed. What was

the school cook doing in her office ninety minutes before lunch? Did she have to fix every little damn thing? "Ask what it's about and schedule him for later this week."

"He's insistent, says he can't leave until he sees you."

"Alright," she sighed. Jackie's staff knew that she rarely sent anyone away—she should stop being so accommodating.

Sam's head poked into her office before the rest of his body followed. "Hello, ma'am." Sam was a handsome, hefty man, with a kind, round face and a tentative smile. His shy grin never seemed to fade away or expand into a full smile, almost as if he were worried that he might offend someone if he changed his expression.

"Have a seat, Sam."

"No, ma'am, I'll stand. Thank you."

Jackie nodded. Let the man stand if he wanted to. "Ma'am," he began, "I have a criminal record—and I don't want to lose my job. Can I explain?"

She nodded again and tightened her jaw. Jackie had an idea of what was coming, but Sam deserved the chance to explain in his own words. He'd been a good employee for five solid years, and if there was anyone on Earth who knew about having a "complicated" history, it was Jackie.

"First off," began Sam, "let me admit that I did fudge things a bit on my application. I'm really sorry, but it was my only hope for gettin' this job... which I think you'll agree I've been pretty good at." He paused for a moment, this confession wasn't easy for him. "I was arrested for marijuana possession in '96. I wasn't dealing, but my friends and I had kicked in for a large bag, two ounces—I was the one got caught holding it. My freebie lawyer tried to get the charge reduced to a misdemeanor, but it didn't happen. I got slapped with a felony and served a year, then did parole with community service. Clean record ever since, though."

Jackie waited for more, but apparently Sam had said his piece. "You're working with children, Sam. Do you think telling the truth now exonerates you from lying on your application?"

"No, ma'am," answered Sam immediately.

"Well then, what is it you imagine I can do for you?" Jackie didn't give a damn about the pot, but lying on his application unexpectedly vexed her. Perhaps it cut just a little too close to the bone.

"Put in a word about my service these last five years? That's all I ask," Sam implored.

"I'll do what I can, but I have no influence on the legal system," replied Jackie. She wondered if she would've been so aggravated over something like this thirty-six hours ago. So he smoked pot as a kid. What man's life should be ruined over that?

"Thank you, ma'am." Jackie expected Sam to leave, but he just kept standing there. Clearly, he had something else to say. After a moment, Sam asked, "Do you have to tell anyone else? I mean before they run the fingerprints through and ...?"

Jackie's aggravation softened a bit. She felt for him— she really did—but she also knew she couldn't be seen as lenient or sympathetic. Sam was a good man, she didn't want to lose him, and she knew he was putting his son through college. Nonetheless, she had protocol to follow.

"I'm sorry, Sam. It's my responsibility to provide this new information to the administration immediately."

"Yes, ma'am." Sheepishly, Sam turned slowly and left her office. He closed the door behind him.

Jackie tried to get back to work, but her concentration had vanished again. *"Let she who is without sin..."* she thought. She'd been raised in the church, after all; some Bible verses had never quite left her.

✥

Driving home, the sour dread in Jackie's heart grew exponentially as she neared her neighborhood. Could she really face Peter?

Two blocks from her house, she pulled into Garfield Park. It was a warm day, and the trees swaying gently in the breeze were beautiful, calming. Jackie had intended to take a walk and steel herself before seeing Peter, but she just sat in the car staring out the window. Two kids, both too young for kindergarten, were tossing a ball back and forth. Twins, it seemed. One brother was being so encouraging, so kind, that she found herself crying. Yep. Her emotional-bullshit-superpower was definitely compromised. She counted backward from ten before driving the last two blocks home.

Jackie closed the door quietly behind her, but Peter had heard her come in nonetheless. "In the kitchen," he called.

Jackie had hoped to sneak upstairs and change out of her work clothes, but there was no point in trying to avoid the unavoidable. She put down her briefcase and headed toward the kitchen. Almost afraid to cross the kitchen's threshold, she stopped and leaned on the doorframe.

Peter, sipping his coffee, was sitting in his usual spot at the table. "There's a fresh pot. And I picked up those ginger muffins you like," he said from behind the newspaper he was pretending to read.

How many pots of coffee had he been through that day? Jackie wondered. Doc Wright had warned him to cut back, but Peter just kept drinking pot after pot. Jackie shook her head to clear it. What an absurd thing to think about in a moment like this. Here she was, about to send her whole marriage crashing down, about to admit her years and years of betrayal, yet she was thinking about acid reflux. In no way did this man, whom she'd always loved despite her lie, deserve what was coming.

Peter pulled the newspaper down from his face and let it fall to the table. He looked his wife directly in the eye. Jackie thought she could still see the hurt from last night in his face, but his next words were bright.

"Good news, Jackie. Helman's ready to sign a contract. Guess he enjoyed seeing you throw that drink in Druid's face. There's always been some tension between those two."

"Glad to be of service." Jackie let her hand trail over Peter's shoulders, then bent to kiss the top of his head. "You didn't need me, after all. You would've got that contract on your own merits."

"I always need you," replied Peter, reaching up and giving her hand a squeeze. "And I know it made a difference that you were there."

Jackie went to the sink and filled the kettle, then set it

on the stove to boil. Tea for her—coffee was the last thing she needed.

"Something's going on at school I need to tell you about," Jackie blurted out. She let the words almost fall out of her mouth—if she didn't get them out now, she never would. "There's a new law requiring all school personnel to be fingerprinted and—"

"I thought we were going to talk about us, about you," Peter frowned.

Jackie grabbed the chair across from him and slowly, deliberately, pulled it away from the table before sitting down. "That's what I'm doing," she said softly but firmly. This is where it starts. You gotta let me tell you in my own way."

Sizing her up, Peter ran his eyes over his wife. Jackie's eyes seemed both softer and two shades darker. That was Jackie's tell—that's how he knew her words were earnest. Finally, Peter leaned over, took a muffin from the plate, sliced it, and said, "To ensure that deadbeats and criminals aren't roaming the halls, good idea."

"It is, of course, but..." Jackie's stomach flipped, her nerves gave out on her. She stood up suddenly, knocking back her chair in the process. "But listen... I've got to get out of this skirt."

"Jackie, stop." Peter's voice was firm but not unkind.

The screech-whistle of the kettle was like an incarnation of the conflict inside of her. She walked over to the stove and tried to pour the hot water into her mug, but splashed it on her blouse instead. "Damn!" she winced. She set the kettle down with a bang, then began blotting her blouse with a dish towel.

Peter rushed over to help. "You burned?" Jackie shook her head in answer. He took the towel from her and folded it in half calmly, then put his hands gently on her shoulders. "Sit," he insisted. "I'll make your tea."

Jackie was about to object when she realized she was trembling. She gave in just a little, righted her chair, and sat back down.

"Whatever it is, it can't be that bad, baby. There's nothing that's going to drive me away. I promise you, Jackie."

"Please don't make a promise you don't know if you can keep." Jackie's words were cracked, dry. She didn't recognize the voice that came from her lips, and she knew Peter didn't either.

The silence that followed hung for several long moments in the air.

"Jackie, this isn't just about school, I know that much," Peter said as he placed a steaming mug in front of her. "Take it slow. Start at the beginning. What's the first thing you need me to know?"

She didn't deserve his patience. Jackie lowered her eyes, her words almost a mumble. "Peter, my name is not Jacqueline Macon."

Peter pressed his lips together into a hard frown. "I thought you were going to be serious, Jackie. This isn't a game."

"No game." She sipped her tea, wishing there was something stronger in her mug. "A long time ago, long before I met you. I left my name behind when I ran away."

Peter looked into his wife's eyes again. They were still two shades darker. He took a deep breath, chose his next two words very carefully. "From Texas?"

"Alabama," whispered Jackie. "My given name is Gloria." Hot, angry, fearful tears escaped from her eyes; moist, silent trails rolled heavily down her checks.

Peter got up from his chair and sat himself next to her. He moved as if he were suddenly thirty years older, as if every ounce of his body were in pain. "How old were you?"

"Seventeen. Decades ago."

Peter took a long, deep breath, which he held for what seemed like an entire month. He closed his eyes, considering. Jackie knew it was only fair to give her husband a moment, but she didn't know how long she could hold out waiting for his reaction. Her trembling became worse.

"That's too many years to make a difference now," Peter finally answered as he took his wife's moist face in his hands, which only mad Jackie cry harder in relief.

He held Jackie's face for yet another long moment. The woman he knew wasn't quite there. Instead, Peter saw a wounded little girl peeking through. The next question, hard as it was, was necessary. "Who hurt you?"

"I got pregnant. Outside of Montgomery. But that's not the worst o—"

"Rape?" he interjected. Peter said it just about as gently as any man could possibly say the word rape, but Jackie couldn't look at him anymore. She pulled her face from his hands.

She nodded once. "White man."

Peter tried to take his wife in his arms, but she resisted. "You're not the criminal, Jackie." *Jackie.* That was her name as far as he was concerned. His Jackie.

Jackie stood up. She wanted some air. Her head was swimming, her stomach was spinning, waves of conflicting emotions crashed over her one by one. Peter hadn't thrown her out, hadn't called her a liar. Hadn't accused her, hadn't left her. Yet for all she'd just told him, he still only knew half the story. Not even half, really.

She'd only taken three or four steps when her knees buckled. Gave out completely. She collapsed onto the floor as a fifty-year-old tidal wave of emotion rose out of her. A stream of tears that wouldn't stop. A stream so thick she couldn't see, couldn't breathe.

Peter on the floor next to her. Peter's arms around her. Peter's damp shirt, speckled with her tears. Peter's voice. What was he saying?

It didn't matter. His words didn't matter, that's not what she needed right now. She surrendered herself, melted into his arms, cried. For one moment at least, she would allow herself to be deeply loved, to feel truly safe.

CHAPTER 5

SUMMER, 1961—ALABAMA

Helen was always the praying kind. The one people called on when family members were ill, when a son was jailed, or when a daughter's belly swelled. She was a praying woman—a knee-to-the-ground, head-to-the-sky, tear-in-her-eye praying woman. She didn't just believe in the power of prayer, she lived it. Which is exactly why Helen wanted her daughter, Gloria, to lead the dinner prayer tonight. Helen needed mountains to move and giants to fall, and right now the best conduit was Gloria. Helen's giant, her husband George, was seated at the other end of the table. The Lord knew Helen tried her best to be a good Christian wife to the man she still loved, but the Lord also knew George hadn't made it easy for her over these last few years.

"Come, Gloria. Lead us in a prayer." Helen prompted.

Helen met Gloria's keen brown eyes with a nod of her head, then smiled widely and blinked rapidly. The two of them had always had a tight bond, a sort of kinetic knowing of each other.

Gloria glanced in turn at her sister Linda, then at her father. Helen could read the nervousness on her daughter's face as Gloria gnawed on her bottom lip.

"Yes ma'am," Gloria said in a sure voice that didn't match the look on her face. Helen stretched her arms out, and each of her daughters slid their palms into hers.

"We gon' have to reheat the food if somebody don't start," George huffed. Since he wasn't a religious man, he had no qualms about his wife leading the nightly prayer. He preferred it, but he also preferred to eat food that wasn't two degrees colder than the fridge.

"Let us pray," began Gloria, before she took a deep breath and bowed her head. Gloria didn't want to pray at dinner. It wasn't that she didn't like praying, it was that she didn't like saying her personal prayers aloud for others to hear. Those words, her words of worry or wonder, were for the Almighty's ears only. But Gloria had a goal. A goal so big that only Jesus could bring it to her.

"Heavenly Father, thank you for your amazing love. Thank you for blessing us with a season of good crops. Thank you, dear God, for granting us the power of mind to make a living. With your grace, Lord, allow us to sell everything we have tomorrow when we go into the city."

"Yes, Jesus," Helen hummed in agreement with her daughter.

"With our earnings, Lord, allow us to buy new dresses for homecoming," Gloria continued.

George cleared his throat loudly. Gloria knew her father was warning her. The rough scratchy noise from her daddy's throat was a clear indication that she was wading into deep water, like a siren that cautioned when she was tipping too close to disrespect.

But Gloria went on. It was her prayer, so she was going to say whatever words she needed to say. "And Lord, help my daddy to see fit in his heart to allow me to go to Montgomery Lab for that two-week course. Lord, you know our hearts. I thank you for your grace, Jesus. I am thankful for the mind that you have given me, and I pray that this prep program will allow me to spread your word even further when I become a teacher someday. In Jesus' name..."

Helen nudged her daughter's leg underneath the table. Gloria understood her mother's hint—she had forgotten the primary purpose of the dinner prayer.

"Oh yes, and thank you for the food we are about to receive for the nourishment for our bodies. In your Holy Name, we pray. Amen."

"Amen." Helen agreed.

"Amen. Amen," Linda chimed in.

George was clearly not happy with his daughter's prayer. She was putting on a show and he knew it. The food was passed around the table in awkward silence.

Although George didn't speak, his silence said volumes. He left Gloria's prayer floating in the air like a rung chicken's feathers. Gloria could almost see her dream drifting into the table and landing there.

Gloria watched as her father spread a pat of butter across his cornbread. Finally, he spoke. "Pass me those greens."

"Sure thing, Daddy," replied Gloria. She infused just a little too much cheer into her voice as she pushed the

greens toward him. Greens were the last thing she had
wanted to hear from her father's lips. She wanted to
hear her father's response to her prayer, to her goal. The
anticipation was killing her.

George grunted as he scooped a leafy helping onto
his plate. Gloria's leg bounced underneath the table. Her
father ate as though she hadn't just borne her soul, as
though she hadn't just announced her life's goals. Her
father had left school after sixth grade; even with her
mother's support, Gloria really didn't know if he would
give his permission. Montgomery Laboratory High
School offered the finest summer teacher preparation
courses in the state; she wondered if that would influence
his decision.

"You did good Helen," George commented between
bites. "Tastes real fine."

Gloria wanted to roll her eyes, but she knew better.
Her father was stalling. He rarely complimented her
mother on anything. He saved any sweet words for sour
situations, and Gloria had witnessed her father's finesse
at work often enough. The man could charm the scales
off a snake, when he had the desire. It was a trait he'd
picked up from his own father.

Gloria's eyes narrowed as she examined her father.
His skin was iced-whiskey brown and contrasted against
the dark waves that smoothed across his head. Working
at the mill and farming the small patch of land he leased
had strengthened his neck, shoulders, and arms—a
strength that inflated his idea of himself.

Gloria had always been different. Everyone in town
knew it. Even though her face was often buried in a

book, anyone who took the time to look would notice her bright, aware eyes. Even when Gloria was an infant, the town's women would speculate about how smart she would grow up to be based on the way her eyes followed every move. "That gal gon' be something," they would say. "Don't nothing move past her without her watching to know." They pursed their lips and clucked with delight anytime she cooed on cue.

Helen couldn't have asked for a better child: smart, kind, diligent, and respectful. Gloria was always at the top of her class, and even took time out to tutor those who had fallen behind. She was good to her sister, patient and nurturing. Helen now smiled at her daughter, encouraging her. The school year had just come to an end; Helen knew the teacher prep course would work in Gloria's favor when she applied to college next year.

"Daddy..." The word peeked out of Gloria's throat like it was scared to come out.

George pushed the greens onto his fork with his cornbread. He didn't acknowledge his daughter, although he knew what she wanted. To George, Gloria had too much of her mother's kind in her words and walk. She was always trying to do something, go somewhere. She wasn't ever satisfied. He didn't care that Gloria's teachers consistently praised her sharp mind and fast reading. Gloria was his daughter: school hadn't done anything for him and it wouldn't do anything for his children, either. Extra schooling would only make Gloria feel higher than she was, which would be nothing but an invitation for the world to beat her back down to her rightful place. A son, maybe, could reach for better, but Helen hadn't given him any sons. And in any case, George had learned a lot about getting beat back into place early in his life. No use for hopes when hell had a high reach.

"What you want?" George replied as harshly. If ignoring Gloria didn't work, then maybe his temper would scare away her notions.

"I want to go to Montgomery," Gloria answered quietly.

"Eat your food," George stated bluntly.

"I want to go to school in Montgomery, Daddy." She said a little louder. Gloria wanted to get her point across, but she didn't want to catch a whipping, either. She'd have to mind her tone as she attempted to reason with her father. "I'm going to be a teacher. You know they have the best programs there."

"More legs open than books is what I hear about the place," George grunted, dismissing his daughter's plea.

Linda took a sharp, audible breath. Her father was by no means a refined man, but vulgarity at the dinner table was rare. People said Linda was the "slow" twin—she was born with her umbilical cord wrapped around her neck—but she knew shame when she heard it. She didn't exactly know what her daddy had meant, yet Linda knew it had something to do with boys and girls touching each other in a way the Lord didn't intend.

Gloria took in a deep breath. "I don't do those things, Daddy, I promise." Gloria had a lot more to say on the matter—she had hardly looked at a boy, even though many of her friends had started dating already. But the strain of holding back her emotions limited her words, "I just want to learn," she managed to add.

George's reply was to pick a bit of meat from between his teeth. He didn't look up; he knew Gloria would have that look of hers. The look of disappointment that made him believe that Gloria wasn't just Gloria, but some otherworldly incarnation of his mother-in-law, his wife, and Gloria herself all meshed into one body. Where did these women get their ambition from? Ain't they seen the world?

Finally, after picking at his teeth for a solid minute, George said, "You go to school, ain't you? You already learning right here in town. Right here, where I can see you." George knew this Montgomery Lab nonsense was Helen's doing, yet the decision remained his—he was still the head of this family. He wished his wife would remember that every now and again.

George's sharp words had cut through the center of Gloria's hope. "It's not the same, Daddy," Gloria appealed. "I can learn more in Montgomery."

"You doing fine just right where you are," George pronounced. "You can stay here, where it don't cost extra."

George's words may have been directed at Gloria, but Helen was his real target and she knew it. Of the many issues in their marriage, their varied backgrounds were a constant source of conflict. They'd come from two very different places in life and, despite their matrimonial union, they'd never quite succeeded in merging the two. Especially where money was concerned.

George had grown up in what Helen thought of as a shack. A shack barely fit for human habitation. The walls were literally propped up with lumber George's father had salvaged from around town. Those beams held up the shack longer than George's father had—the man had disappeared when George was young, just after his sister, eleven years younger, had been born. That's when George had learned that he and his mother were his father's second family. George's mother was, in effect, a second wife. A *secondary* wife. That's why they were so poor; George's father provided for his "real" family first, then tossed George's mother the scraps.

Helen's people certainly weren't rich, but they were a good bit better off, and her parents were husband and wife, just like the Lord intended. They had struggled to make the bills sometimes, but struggling was the exception, not the rule, and Helen's family faced challenges together. Helen had been taught to strive for more, whereas for George marrying Helen and purchasing their shotgun house was more—all the *more* he would ever strive for. He had done better than his father, and that was enough. If she'd given him a son, Helen often thought George might be fully contented.

Helen broke in before Gloria could respond, "George, surely you know the schools around here don't offer half of the classes Gloria needs to start her degree." Helen wanted to add that even the government had finally broken down and admitted that all schools were not created equally, but she took another route instead. "It's only two weeks, and you can't put a price on knowledge."

George grunted and sucked at his teeth. "The toilets she gon' end up scrubbing after she finishes school ain't gon' be singing songs just 'cause she learned all them fancy numbers and big words." Whatever little patience George had was rapidly coming to an end. "You know better than anybody: you went to college, but you ain't got no fancy job. Them papers don't change skin!"

"Mrs. Stinson said I could be a great teacher," Gloria interjected. The familiar tension between her parents was now hanging in the air; her words were to diffuse the situation as much as to make her point.

"It's true Daddy, she did say that. I heard." Linda chimed in with an innocent, proud smile on her face. "When Mama and me met Gloria after school, I heard." Linda liked telling the truth; she always lit up eagerly when she had a simple truth to tell.

The high school had refused to take Linda; they said she was too slow and needed a special school in Montgomery, the family couldn't afford the dorm fees. But Helen sometimes brought her daughter to meet Gloria after classes ended for the day. Linda needed some time to socialize with girls her own age, and Gloria's schoolmates, especially her friend Vivian, always treated Linda kindly.

It was just around the time Linda had left school that George had begun pulling away. As hard as Helen had prayed on it, she'd never worked out what one had to do with the other, but nor had she figured out any other cause. In a way it didn't matter: Helen would always look after her babies regardless of George's feelings on the matter. Her children came first; even the pastor had counseled her as much.

George looked at Linda for a moment, then back to Gloria. Suddenly switching to his charming voice, he said, "It ain't like Montgomery Lab's around the corner, Glowbug."

Gloria winced at the nickname, and George's smooth tone agitated her even more. Her father only called her *Glowbug* when he was trying to charm her, when he wanted something. That *something* could be as minor as behaving herself in public, or as huge as keeping his secrets. Gloria knew her father did more on weekends than toss back a few drinks at the local shot house; she often supposed that he had inherited infidelity from his own father, as if it were a trait that could be passed down in the blood.

"Things are changing all over, Daddy. The Southern Christian Leadership gon' be five years old this coming winter, and Reverend King's doing all kinds of good work, even from Atlanta. Pretty soon, Negroes will be able to do jus' about anything, and I want to be ready."

"She does have a point, George. Remember the bus boycott? Things ain't the same as when we were young," Helen added. "The world will change one way or the other, why can't it be for the better? I pray on it every night."

Gloria jumped back in before he father could respond. "An' Mrs. Stinson says I have more potential than any student she's taught in a long time. She believes in me, Daddy. Why don't you?"

Anger flared in George's eyes. He was now done with this foolishness. Damn women were ganging up on him in his own home, and it was Friday night—he had somewhere to be. He grabbed Gloria's plate and held it up to her face.

"Did Mrs. Stinson buy this food? Is Mrs. Stinson gon' pay for them homecoming dresses with her good teacher check?"

"No, but—"

"Then Mrs. Stinson don't have any say in what you do or who you become," George bellowed. "I don't give a lick—"

Helen broke in. "Mrs. Stinson already found a family who's willing to open their home to Gloria," she said firmly. Her husband was on the verge of storming off from the table, but she needed to get this last point across. "Good church folk with two daughters themselves. Normal folk who are willing to take in our girl while she betters herself."

George looked at Helen with a dare in his eyes. "Sound like you not asking my permission. Sound like you already know what you gon' do."

Gloria was close to tears. She wanted to hide under her bed and have a good cry, just like when she was a child. Across the table, Linda, clearly scared by their father, *was* crying. Gloria managed to catch her eye, which soothed her sister some. As twins, they could sometimes communicate more with just a glance than with a whole paragraph full of words.

Gloria fought back her own anger, her own burning tears. When Mrs. Stinson had told her about the teacher-prep opportunity, Gloria knew she had to try. Even if she knew her father would hit the roof. Even if Montgomery was at least a forty-five minute drive away. She turned again to her father and, while minding her tone, pleaded, "I knew you wouldn't let me go unless I had a plan, Daddy. Mrs. Stinson even said that some of the churches might help with the cost."

George answered with a face nearly as steeled as his

words. "You know I need you here helping your mama. And I just tol' you Mrs. Erma Stinson ain't have no say. Favorite teacher or not. You *my* daughter.

"But Daddy, it's—"

"An' maybe you should spend less time listenin' to the likes of Reverend King and more time listenin' to your own father! You think this world gon' change jus' cause some young preacher say so? Your skin is my skin, no changin' that. No matter how many damn books you read."

Helen glared at her husband as he stormed away. Her heart ached, physically ached. The hard-hearted, pigheaded man who'd just left his family in the middle of dinner was not the same man she married years ago.

CHAPTER 6

George felt like his life wasn't his own. If the sun was up, so was he. Monday through Friday, he labored hour after hour at Sawyer's Wood Mill, often until his fingers bled. The wood gin he made earned him his main paycheck, but when the sun went down and George arrived home, his day wasn't finished: he still had to work the plot of land he leased, all so he could make just enough money to be broke. Between his wife and two daughters, the money he earned flew away faster than sawdust on a windy day. Only on Friday night did George feel like he owned his life. This was the one moment in the week, a precious few hours, when he laid all his tools aside and his aches dulled away.

"Where you going?" Helen shouted at George's back through the screen door of their home. After he'd stormed off from the dinner table, George had gone to bathe and shave. He'd changed into a pair of sleek pants and a button-down shirt. A few minutes later, he was heading out the door.

Although Helen's words sounded like a question, they were anything but. She knew exactly where George was going, and she knew why he'd left looking so sharp. As a newlywed, her aunt had told her that a married woman had three options: stay two steps ahead of her man, know where her man was stepping, or be stepped on herself. Nothing could be more true in her marriage now. Yet knowing what her husband did with his Friday nights didn't change the pain Helen felt, only the way she approached him. She purposefully asked questions to tug at his guilt. If he had any guilt left— Helen wasn't exactly sure her husband was capable of feeling guilty anymore.

"I'll be back," George answered without even turning around.

Swallowing back a lump of pain that was now knotted in her throat, Helen mumbled, "I knew that." George always came back home. George came back home and tortured everyone with his frustrations, barked at the twins in irritation, and left for Helen a loneliness in his wake instead of love. George always came back home, that much was true, but Helen knew that he didn't want to come home. He'd rather be drinking. He'd rather be whoring with that young gal of his.

※

George's battered truck rumbled down the dark road that led deep into the backwoods at the edge of the county. The road was little more than a path, and the forest was dense. The trees clasped together in an arch above so tightly that the evening sky was barely visible as he drove.

George reached under the seat and again pulled out his stash of corn liquor. He took his fourth or fifth good swig; the booze was doing its job nicely. He had been waiting all week for this, and his family's drawn-out dinner had both tested his patience and deprived him of the little free time he had to himself.

After a few more minutes and a few more swings from his bottle, George spotted his destination in the clearing ahead: a long, white, clapboard house. Whatever vice gripped a man, he could find the cure at Black Gal's Place. The house, with its wide, stilted porch, beckoned the frustrated, the beat down, and the broken. On Friday nights Black Gal's was usually full to its bends with folks trying to forget what the week before had brought—and what the week ahead held in store. But George didn't go to Black Gal's just to blow off steam, he went for the company of one woman in particular.

Usually, the clearing was packed with cars, but tonight only a few vehicles littered the makeshift parking lot. George barely noticed, though—he was feeling too good from the liquor. He got out of his truck and squished across the damp, red-clay-path like a man on a mission. The woman he so longed to see wasn't waiting for him on the porch. He was sober enough to notice that.

The wooden screen door squeaked open as George banged his smooth black shoe against the threshold. "Where the hell everybody at?" George barked over the jukebox's sultry music. He didn't see his woman—the woman that he wanted to be near at all times—in the front room, either. Worry boiled in his gut: Vera was always waiting for him.

Although tonight's crowd was thin, all were regulars. They went on drinking, eating, and dancing as if George hadn't spoken. They all knew George was asking a question that only Black Gal could answer, and no one was foolish enough to answer for Black Gal. She was not that type of woman.

"Where the hell everybody at?" George hollered again. No one missed the slurring in his words. The room's collective refusal to reply cut into George; every day of his life he harbored the fear that Vera would one day take off and go on with her life. He was a married man: perhaps one day, Vera would get tired of waiting.

Stella stepped out of the kitchen and smoothed her hands over the hips that had mesmerized many a man. Her hazel-green eyes narrowed at George. What right did he have to question any business of Black Gal's? And what kind of nerve did he have, showing up here tonight?

"Everybody at the same place your balls are," Stella's voice was small, but it carried in a big way—it sliced right through the general commotion of the room. "They home with they wife."

Stella was Black Gal's housemate and business partner, but most folks suspected there was something more between them. Whatever the case, they were an odd pair. Black Gal was a towering, wide woman with a withering glare—an ocean of forcefulness unto herself— while Stella was petite, all lava and popping with spitfire. She lured people in with her mysterious eyes and curvaceous body, but could just as easily cut folks down with her slicing words and strong left hook.

"Stella! Don't!" Vera cried out just as the small but

forceful woman was about to slap George for showing up so drunk. "I know my mama said—"

"He don't need to be messing with you," Stella fumed. Black Gal had never been exactly happy about Vera's instance on seeing George, and Black Gal was still fuming after last week's incident. Stella always made sure Black Gal's feelings were known, especially when it came to George.

"Quit trying to turn her against me!" George yelled.

Stella's lip twitched with fury as her fists clenched. She took a deep breath. "You can do much better than this old, shriveled, hand-me-down man," she said, trying to reason with Vera.

"You bulldagger bitch!" George yelled as he pulled Vera toward him. "Stay out of my business."

"Your business is in your own house. With your wife. Not with a gal half your age." Stella snarled.

"Not in here!" Black Gal boomed as she appeared from the hall. All movement in the place stopped. There was no way to ignore Black Gal or her orders. No one even tried.

"I ain't got time for this shit," Stella muttered. She shot forward like a bull, gave George a good shove with her shoulder, and kept on moving straight out the front door.

Black Gal moved forward and eyed George. "If you wasn't so drunk, I'd kick your ugly ass out," she grumbled. "I told you I ain't want to see you here this weekend."

"I got it, Mama. I'll take care of it," pleaded Vera.

Black Gal only glared at Vera. She didn't want her

daughter anywhere near George. The two had taken up together three years ago, and she'd been telling Vera all that time to get herself away from him. But here her daughter was, defending George again.

Black Gal growled. George was the type of man that she couldn't stand: the kind of man that smiled a bit too friendly at little girls a third of his age, watched them until they blossomed, and then destroyed their bloom. Black Gal couldn't bear the way he hounded after Vera in the night, then cowered from her and the baby during the day. Last weekend, when Black Gal had caught the two of them nearly naked in a back room, things had finally come to a head. She'd told Vera outright that George wasn't welcome on Friday and Saturday nights, when she had a business to run.

A slight breeze cooled around Black Gal as she stepped onto the porch "Vera, get his drunk ass some coffee so he can sober up and get the hell out my house," she ordered through the screen door. Vera moved George to the kitchen. "And check on them greens, too," Black Gal added.

Stella's slim, shapely figure emerged from the surrounding darkness. Black Gal had wanted to stay angry, but Stella made her feel like the taste of warm maple syrup.

"Sherriff still down the way, jus' waiting," Stella reported as she stepped onto the porch. "You know he got to make his roundup look real good."

Black Gal nodded, but didn't say anything.

"Joyce?" Stella asked as she searched Black Gal's face. "What's worrying you?"

People had called Black Gal names all of her life, none of which she had chosen. Black Gal was called *Nazarene* by the woman who birthed, but then abandoned, her. She was called *Gal* by her grandmother, who hadn't liked Black Gal's birth name. *Fat Gal* soon followed by the neighborhood kids. Finally, *Black Gal* is what took. Stella was the only one person who ever thought Black Gal should be named something pretty, something that reflected Black Gal's true dignity. That's why Stella called her *Joyce*.

"Sherriff Daniels won't be a problem," Stella comforted. We've known about the raid for days. This is all for show. He'll take his ten gallons of corn liquor, then we'll pay to get it back, jus' like all them other times. The house is 'bout empty anyhow. Most folks had the good sense to stay home, once we got word out." Stella paused for a moment. "And if he come too close to finding something he shouldn't, I'll distract him. He got an eye for me anyway."

Black Gal didn't respond; she just kept watching the night. Stella was right, in a way. This was all for show—the sheriff himself had told them when he was coming and what he'd be confiscating. But Black Gal also knew that no one could ever really be ready for Sheriff Daniels: the lawman of Lowndes County was as dirty as the mud on a pig farm.

Stella moved closer to Black Gal and caressed her cheek. Black Gal relaxed a measure, knowing Stella would do whatever it took to make her feel protected. Black Gal liked that about the woman. No man, neither kin nor lover, had ever claimed Black Gal the way Stella had. No man had ever been as loyal or as loving. Black Gal had been alone in the world—alone for a long, long time before Stella came along.

"Talk to me," Stella said softly as she took Black Gal by the hand. "That ol' fool and Vera... that's what's pullin' at you?"

"I want to kill him." Black Gal confessed. She look up and watched the twinkle of the stars rather than facing the concern in Stella's eyes. "I hate what he done to my daughter," Black Gal admitted. "And I told him to stay away. He want to see the baby during the week, sober, that's one thing. But drunk like that? When he *know* we being raided tonight? That's disrespecting Vera, and disrespecting what I've built here. I want to shoot him, hang him by the ankles, skin him slow."

"Well, with all that liquor in him... we can take him," Stella joked, but Black Gal didn't laugh. She had meant all her words. The part about her business, yes, but the part about Vera even more so. As far as she was concerned, George had defiled her child—a married man who preyed on her daughter with his false sweetness. It was torture to watch her daughter, whom she'd brought up to expect better for herself, fall victim to a man old enough to be her father, a man who could never marry her.

Even more frustrating was that Black Gal knew she didn't have a choice in the matter, not if she wanted to keep her daughter close. Vera had always been the brighter side of life to Black Gal—her child was the better days and kinder nights that could still come someday. She couldn't bear to lose the last piece of sweetness left in her life.

"He got a wife and two girls at home. What he need with Vera?" Black Gal began. "I didn't raise her to be some man's outside woman. I didn't raise her to have a lowlife's child out of wedlock. While he was sittin' stupid in his home with Helen, she was giving birth alone. She was giving birth the same way I brought her to this world, and the same way my mama gave me life: without a man beside her." Black Gal choked back emotion. She sometimes allowed herself to be soft with Stella, but she wouldn't cry in front of anyone.

"Her life isn't over Joyce. Shit, she ain't but twenty-one, and little Michael's barely two years old. She can still find a good man to take her and have a good life," Stella offered.

"Not with George around. I see it in her eyes. She look at him like candy, like he a prize." Black Gal sighed. "I thought I was starting to get through to her these last months. That baby getting older now, it only gon' get harder to find a man who'll have them. Lord know George ain't care for 'em. I thought—"

"You can't worry about that," Stella replied. "You trained her up in the way she should go. She's strayed a bit, but she'll find the right path again, sooner or later."

Before Black Gal could respond, her three hired men walked up to the porch. Avery, James, and Two Sticks had all come to Black Gal at different times, but all for the same reason: work. When a young man in the county got himself a record, he lost far more than the time he spent behind bars—there wasn't a mill or factory for miles that would hire a colored man with a record, at least not at a livable wage. As employees of Black Gal, the men earned a decent wage plus some.

"Everything that needed putting away is locked up tight," Avery reported. He was a smooth guy with a kind heart and rough hands.

"Anything else you need for us to do?" James asked.

Black Gal pushed back her emotion and slid into boss mode. "Nothing right now," she answered. "Soon as the sheriff leave, business gon' be back to normal. You know how some of them Negroes get to actin' when they got a little money and some liquor in them."

The men each cracked a smile. They had been around Black Gal's long enough to know what Friday night looked like. Never a dull moment.

"If you don't mind, we'll head on out 'til then. Ain't no use in us meeting with the law unless we have to," James said.

"I second that," Avery supported. Two Sticks nodded in agreement.

Black Gal cocked her head. "Just make sure you back."

"Thank you," the three men said in unison. After a pause, Two Sticks added, "I don't say it much, but I thank you for everything you done for me, ma'am."

The others agreed with nods of their heads before disappearing into the night.

"You a good woman, Joyce," Stella soothed, brushing the side of Black Gal's arm. "I know it and they do too. You hard, but you good—and you've helped all kind of people in this life, no matter the trouble that's found them. All them women. Everything will work itself right on out."

CHAPTER 7

The sheriff's black and white squad car, now filled with a good portion of Black Gal's booze, crawled over the red dirt like a roach in the sun. All Black Gal could do was watch as her livelihood was carried away.

In her mind, Black Gal calculated the amount of money she'd lose for the week. She hated this part of her business. A payoff to the sheriff and his cronies guaranteed her protection against the local law, but the payments were painful. With the amount she'd lost, she'd have nothing to put into *run fund* this week; that vexed her more than anything.

"Alright ya'll... they gone now," Black Gal said as she looked out the doorway at the retreating lawmen. "They made it real fast this time."

"Yup. They made off with that whole pot of greens too," said Stella, a hand on her hip.

"He did what?" Black Gal yelled. She spun around with a speed that was surprising for a woman her size. She had to look her Stella in the face to make sure the words she had just spoken were real. "He took my greens?"

"His low-down deputy, yeah. Claimed he needed to check the pot to see what we was cooking," Stella replied. Black Gal's Place was known as much for her cooking as it was for the moonshine. Her greens in particular were a favorite. Bacon fat *and* a ham hock—that was her secret.

"He knew what the hell was in that pot," Black Gal spat. "Damn fool, always making trouble. So that's why he run out so fast."

Black Gal slammed the screen door behind her with so much force that the whole house shook. "Vera!" she yelled. The room's chatter and music were no match for Black Gal's booming voice.

"Yes, Mama?" answered Vera as she ran out of the kitchen.

"We down on liquor, and now we ain't got a lot of greens we can cook, neither." Black Gal shook her head. "Go out and pull up some more. We gon' push them chicken plates tonight to make up some money."

Vera's shoulders slumped. She hated picking collards with a passion, but she always did it for her mother. Tonight, she would drag herself out into the insect-filled darkness with a flashlight and dig around in the dirt until she found the best leafy plants.

Vera went back into the kitchen and wiped her hands on a dishrag. If she had to go out in the fields, at least it would give her a few moments alone with George. She took George by the hand, led him out the back door, then down the old wooden steps.

"I sure like the way you move," George slurred. Vera had been pumping coffee into him for a good hour, but

George still wasn't fully sober. Which was good in a way; George enjoyed being buzzed. Vera knew George liked his moonshine almost as much as he liked her—which was saying something, because George liked Vera a lot.

Vera liked George too—she had ever since he first started smiling her way. Young men her age were always rough and impatient, whereas George was smooth and nurturing. He wooed her, made her smile, and he doted on their son whenever he was able to get away from his wife.

The ground was cool as Vera pushed her hands into the earth. Damn collards were low plants. Hard enough to get to 'em by day, never mind at night. "You gon' get yourself killed coming over here and talking crazy," she warned as she searched for the best plants.

"Black Gal all talk," George huffed as he bolted upright. He then attempted to steady himself on the uneven ground. Nope, he was not even close to sober.

Vera straightened and looked him in the eye. "No, she ain't. She knows people," she replied. When folks weren't acting right in Black Gal's eyes, Vera knew her mother had a way of bringing on untold misfortunes to get them back in line. "You a fool of a man sometimes, George. You best start listening to my mama."

Vera went back to picking, but she didn't get far before George pulled her body back against his. His hand slid around her thighs then locked between her legs for a moment, before he effectively fitted the curve of her backside against his hardness.

"You ain't think this foolish last week," George joked as he swiveled his hips and pressed himself into her.

"I got stuff to do," Vera fussed. She pulled away from George, but she knew that when he got himself fired up, there was only way to get him out of it. But she wasn't about to do that out in the open in her mother's field, especially after last week.

George spun her around and pulled her close again. Vera placed a hand on his muscled chest to push him away, but her attempt lacked conviction. His muscles felt too good beneath her fingertips.

"I need to finish picking these greens," Vera murmured.

"I pick you. Here, let me rub that dirt off." George charmed. He rubbed at Vera's backside with his strong hands. He slid an arm around Vera's waist and hooked her body against his before kissing her lips.

Vera didn't come to him easily, but then she relaxed into the kiss and fell into the rush that ignited every time George touched her. But when George crooked his finger into the waistband of her skirt and started tugging it downward, she knew she had to push him away. Black Gal would do more than sick Stella on him if she ever caught the two of them together again.

"We got to stop," Vera moaned. "My mama will be wondering what's taking us so long. She'll come out here after me, you know she will."

"Well, I'm not worrying myself 'bout your mama. I'm wanting you," George cooed in Vera's ear. "One day, you will be my wife."

Vera tensed. She hated that subject. George had been talking of wedding bells since before little Michael was born. Over two years later, Vera was still living in her mother's home without a man of her own. Her mother's recent counsel had been having some effect, and Vera had begun wondering a bit about her future.

"When?" Vera asked as she took another step back. She knew George wouldn't give her a straight answer, but that didn't stop her from asking.

"Soon, soon," George stuttered as he tried to close the distance between them. "You know I got the twins at home, and Linda… has troubles. But I love you, Vera. You and Michael, ya'll keep me alive. And I'm gon' be with you someday. Man and wife."

George reached out to touch her face, but Vera leaned away. "Don't do that," she said in a firm, solemn voice. The excitement and tingles from George's touch had withered away.

"Don't do what?" George chuckled nervously. "Touch you? I thought you liked when I touch you."

Vera's anger rose. Why did he have to do that—talk about marriage? She had believed in George, she had trusted him to take her, keep her, and love her for real. She had expected him to keep his promise and leave Helen. Vera had expected him to marry her. While she hadn't brought herself to leave George, she was done expecting. The last thing she wanted to hear were more empty promises.

"Let me touch you," begged George, reaching his hand forward.

"No." Vera slapped his hand away with more force than she intended. "Not when the hand you're touching me with has another woman's wedding ring on it."

George looked at his hand as though he'd never seen

it before, as if his wedding ring had materialized out of thin air. A grown man with two grown daughters staring at his wedding ring in the middle of a field in darkness of night. Vera wondered if George were really as stupid as he looked; how had she never seen this in him before?

"Where my greens?" Black Gal hollered from the porch. "Get in here, Vera."

Vera jogged into the house, leaving George in the field. She wasn't exactly running to her mother, more away from the man who had stolen her heart.

Grease popped off the hot pan as Vera entered the kitchen and dropped the collards near the sink. Black Gal looked at her daughter with harsh eyes.

"What's wrong with your face?" Black Gal asked.

Vera sniffed. She hadn't wanted her mother to notice her tears. Vera couldn't bear to hear her mother gloat about being right: George was never leaving his wife—she'd honestly never realized that before. Not until she saw the fool staring at his wedding ring.

"I'm fine, Mama." Vera turned her face from her mother's gaze. She moved over to the sink and began rinsing the greens. Like any mother, Black Gal knew when her child was hurting, but she also saw an opportunity.

George banged through the porch door. "Vera, I'm sorry," he pleaded. "Vera..."

Black Gal stepped in George's path to allow her daughter time to escape into the front room. "Ya'll been out there fooling around?" Black Gal demanded. "Messing around with my daughter don't pay no bills. And Lord knows you don't give no money for your own son. Why you keep showing up here with your empty promises and sweet words is beyond me. You want my daughter, get her a ring. You twins is grown now, an' just about everyone in the county knows you ain't brought nothing but misery to Helen since little Michael come. Be a man or leave this place for good!"

CHAPTER 8

Helen didn't want to get up. She wanted to stay wrapped up in the bounty of fabric that had held her and kept her warm far more often than her husband had in recent years.

"Gotta get up," she mumbled to herself. As in most instances in her adult life, there was no one there to quiet the concerns that were already spinning in her mind. Just like every other day, her thoughts were awake before she was.

As always, Helen began her morning with a silent prayer. She thanked the Lord for the day, told him her joys and her woes. When her prayers were finished, the comfort of the massive quilt kept Helen anchored to the worn mattress, even though the morning was warm. Years ago, before Helen and George were married, Mama Tee had given the large, padded quilt to Helen as a gift for her hope chest.

Helen slid a finger along the quilt's thick black stitches. Her fingertips knew the quilt so well that she could tell by touch the spots where her grandmother had been angry while sewing—the small, short strokes gave it away. In other places, the stitches were calm and evenly spaced, and Helen could imagine Mama Tee humming as she carefully pushed the needle through the material.

When Mama Tee had given her the quilt, she'd told Helen that a wife could make great use of a needle. In her youth, Helen had taken the comment as an insult: she thought her grandmother was telling her that women should only cook, sew, and birth babies—not go off to college with big dreams. It wasn't until much later that Helen realized Mama's Tee wisdom. As the years passed, Helen learned that her thimble and needle were a salve for angst and a station where her always-moving mind could stop for a rest.

Helen swung her still-sleepy legs away from the bed and slid her feet into a pair of powder blue slippers. A familiar tightness filled her chest as she rose—it happened most mornings now, this heaviness in her heart, the weight of sleeping next to a man who'd turned so cold. She slid out of the bed carefully, slowly. She had to put a good deal of effort into not waking George.

A gurgled snore vibrated from George's nose. The horrible noise prompted Helen to look over at the man who she had fallen in love with over two decades ago and scrunch her face in disgust. Helen knew what George had been up to the night before by the way he smelled— wild onions, musk-rose, corn liquor. He'd come home fairly early last night, but she knew who he'd been with all the same. Worse, Gloria had heard him come in drunk; Helen was sure of it.

There were days when Helen wanted to shake good sense into his brain. How could George be so thick as not to recognize the blessing of a loving family? Then there were days when Helen just wanted him to sleep so that she could be at peace. No arguing. No explanations. None of his tired, overused lies to cover his absences. No need to pray for the strength to be his wife. No need to ask Jesus to bring her real husband back to her.

The day ahead was long. Every spring, Helen and the girls began selling goods from the farm. On Saturdays, they would drive the miles into Montgomery with baskets of wild, fresh-picked plums, full tomatoes, and ample-sized peppers. Crates of chickens ready for new coops rounded out their offerings.

Helen's feet moved through her home, but her mind stayed with her husband. Her heart sent out a prayer for him to become a better man. "Change him, Lord. Change my husband into a man who is great in your eye," she chanted to herself in a rhythm that mimicked her footsteps. "Lead my husband back to a righteous path, Jesus."

Helen believed in redemption. She had seen men change. It had taken the wrath of God and the threat of meeting their maker face-to-face before some of them changed, but she still believed. She believed George could again be the good man that she married, if he would just open his heart to the Lord, if he would let Jesus heal the mysterious rot that had crept into him.

"Get up girls," Helen said encouragingly as she walked into her daughters' room. She pulled back Gloria's covers. "We got a long day yet."

Gloria sat up and sleepily and nodded her head. "Alright, Mama," she yawned. "Linda and I will be out directly. I'll help her get ready, you don't have to worry."

"Mo'mama," came Linda's sleepy voice. *Mo'mama* was Linda's word for "Good morning, Mama." Helen had worked hard over the years to improve her daughter's speech and vocabulary, but she never corrected *mo'mama*. Helen looked forward to hearing it each morning.

Helen felt no small amount of pride as she walked into the kitchen; she could always count on Gloria to look after Linda. The patience and care Gloria took with her sister never ceased to warm Helen's heart. These days, it helped with the ache.

The refrigerator in Helen's home held plenty of eggs. Every Saturday she ritually boiled six of those eggs, two for herself and two for each of her daughters. George could fend for himself later; Saturday mornings with the girls were hers.

In fact, Helen loved Market Day, despite the heavy work of loading and unloading her goods. She enjoyed being with her daughters, she enjoyed Montgomery, she enjoyed earning money for the household, and she enjoyed being away from the husband who didn't want her. Market Day was freedom. One day soon, she hoped to cut Market Day in half so she could take Gloria on a tour of Alabama State. She'd been saving a few coins here and there to add to that day's earnings so that when she did slip away, George would never know she had cut Market Day short. She'd already prayed on it.

When Helen heard the shuffle of heavy footsteps behind her, she didn't even bother to turn around. "Are you ready girls?" she asked, feeling freer by the moment.

"Yea," grumbled George in his thick morning voice.

Helen nearly broke the egg she was holding. She spun around with a fierce quickness. "George!" she choked out. "Why are you awake?" She took in the sight of her disheveled husband. His usually slicked and waved hair was mashed against his head in two opposing directions, and his bloodshot eyes looked sallow against his ashen skin. He was a sight, but she couldn't deny that she still loved him. No matter what George did, the beating of Helen's heart still always sped up—even if her head knew better.

"A man can't be awake in his own house?" George growled as he took a seat at the table.

Helen added two more eggs to the water, and wished with all her might that George hadn't got out of bed simply to eat. "You usually sleep in while me and the girls are off for Montgomery. It's your only day to get a little extra rest." Helen spoke the words calmly, even though her insides were shaking in equal measures of hope and fear at the thought of what George's presence this early in the morning might mean.

"Well, I figured I'd go with ya'll this morning. Ya know, help out." George explained, as if going to the Montgomery market was the most usual thing in the world. As if it hadn't been years since George had come along to spend the day with his family.

Helen examined her husband. She wasn't going to allow herself to expect too much. She didn't want to trust that her husband truly wanted to participate in her life. "You really want to come with us?" Helen asked. "You want to come help me with the girls?"

George leaned back against his chair and folded his arms across his chest. He clicked his teeth. "What? Ya'll don't need me now?" he asked, sounding—to Helen's ears—genuinely hurt.

Helen could hardly believe what she'd detected in her husband's tone, but she didn't stop to acknowledge it. In that moment, all Helen could think about was having her husband with her. Her real husband, the man she had married years ago.

"Yes," Helen began, before stepping toward the man that she had prayed for, "we need you. Of course we need you."

George leaned back in his chair and allowed his arms to relax.

"I just thought—" Helen began.

"Thought what?" George snapped.

Helen was thankful for her husband's help. She didn't want him to change his mind. Extra hands to carry the load and an extra pair of eyes to watch over Linda sounded real nice. Those crates seemed heavier and heavier these days, sometimes it even was hard for her to draw her breath properly.

"I thought it would be good for you to spend time with us," Helen answered sweetly.

George didn't smile, but he didn't grunt or curse, either. Helen was pleased with that.

"I'm gon' get the chickens loaded up." George announced as he stood up from the table. "Make sure the girls get themselves ready."

When the screen door banged shut, Helen smiled.

"Lord, you move in mysterious ways," she mumbled to herself. She trusted that her prayer had moved her husband in the right direction.

❋

"We jus' about sold out!" cried Helen as she smiled and looked over at the twins. She loved it when they could sell everything. It was good for the family's budget, and it generally made George a little less stingy over the week to come.

"It's really all gone?" Linda asked, as she looked at the empty baskets Helen and Gloria were carrying.

"Yes, baby. Empty crates," answered Helen in a sing-song voice.

Linda's eyes brightened. She loved the song Helen had made up for two girls when they were small. Gloria didn't sing along with her mother and sister much anymore, but because today's success meant that they could buy their homecoming dresses, she made an exception.

"Empty crates, no empty plates. Empty truck, we had good luck." The three ladies sang.

Gloria kept the beat on her basket as they made their way back to the truck. They had sold everything but the throw-aways—a basket of goods they had scraped together from the last remains of each of the other baskets. The throw-aways would become stew for tonight's dinner. Stew was an easy dinner; Helen and Linda could do the cooking so Gloria could have an hour or two to herself to read.

"Looks like things went well for your father, too," said Helen as she inspected the empty cages that once held their chickens.

"Got rid of all them birds," George nodded. "We done for the day." He opened the bed of their pick-up truck.

The three ladies and George stood in the parking lot together, but their minds were worlds apart. The girls were dreaming about their new dresses, while the adults were thinking about their profits. Linda smiled as colors and lace twirled around in her mind.

Gloria was just as excited as Linda, even though she kept her joy corked up and away from the others. She imagined how beautiful she would look in the red dress she had seen in the window of Buster's Department Store. She could almost see the jealousy stamped on the other girls' turned-up faces: she would be the best-dressed person at homecoming. Gloria wasn't vain by nature, it was just that she loved homecoming almost as much as she loved her books.

"Empty crates, no empty plates. Empty trucks, we had good luck," Linda began singing again. Linda still found joy in all manner of games and songs, although— at sixteen years old—other girls her age had long lost interest in children's things.

"Hush that noise," George scoffed. "Gloria, you and your sister get the last of the baskets loaded. We be ready to go directly."

Linda's eyes turned toward her father's as her eyebrows pushed together in confusion.

"Our dresses, Mama?" she questioned.

"Yes, baby," Helen replied as she helped her

husband stack the cages, but George didn't so much as peep at Linda's question. In all the years Helen had known George, he always had something to say, even more so when it came to spending money. His silence said more than any sentence he could utter.

"Alright, let's get home," said George as he opened the driver's side door.

"Daddy, we ain't ready to go home yet," Gloria reminded her father. She hadn't thought anything about her father's silence, except maybe that he was getting old and forgetful. She reminded him nicely, "We're going to buy us a dress for homecoming."

"Buy us a dress for homecoming," Linda echoed.

"Where did ya'll get money from?" George replied coolly. Black Gal had scared the dickens out of him last night. If nothing else, he needed to start giving Vera at least a few dollars a week for their son: that money had to come from somewhere. What did the girls need new dresses for anyway?

Gloria looked at her mother. She needed Helen to say something on her behalf. George didn't believe in questions from children about adult decisions—he said it was disrespectful—and after last night's dinner, she didn't dare risk setting him off again.

Gloria looked in her mother's eyes with a silent plea for her help. Helen cleared her throat as the four of them stood still and waited. "We were going to use this week's earning to buy some new dresses, George." Helen explained.

George laughed. "Ya'll get in this truck," he said, dismissing the women's pleas. "We ain't made much today. Ain't no money for dresses. This money is for bills."

Helen shook her head. "That can't be right George." Helen spoke slowly as she calculated in her mind how much money they should have made. "We sold well today. There should be plenty for the girls."

George didn't bother to answer his wife. He turned to the twins instead—an argument he knew he could win. "What you need dresses for? You got dresses."

Tears were knocking at the back of Gloria's eyes. She would look haggard in an old dress. She had already worn last year's dress on a few occasions—everyone would know if she and Linda didn't have something new for homecoming. In a way, she wanted the dresses even more than Montgomery Lab, since Linda deserved a new dress, too.

Linda looked at Gloria, and Gloria looked at Helen.

"You know homecoming is next weekend," Helen reasoned. "The girls help us all year long, and this the one time they get to have something new."

George winced. "Ya'll don't know nothing about hard work." He turned away from the women who loved him. "Come on and get in this truck."

Linda let her tears fall in silence as they piled into the cabin of the old pick-up truck. Gloria balled her fists, but she refused to cry. They sat crammed together, all four across the cabin, in a pall of silence.

After a moment, George spoke across the girls to Helen. "That's the problem. They spend too much money. Boys could earn something here or there, but girls ain't do nothing but take."

"The girls need dresses, George." Helen explained with a firmness in her tone. "They're bigger than they used to be, and they're not children anymore—they need to be presented as young ladies."

George couldn't fight that logic, so he quieted for a slight moment as he considered what to say next. Then he announced, "Helen, you can make the girls two nice dresses," as if he were being gracious. As if clothing his daughters decently were some great favor. As if the girls wouldn't be ridiculed for wearing *mama made* dresses.

Helen stared at the man that God had given her. Her heart ached and the lining of her stomach turned.

CHAPTER 9

elen flitted through her house on the Saturday before homecoming like an over-caffeinated hummingbird. There was so much to do, and it always felt like there was not enough time. Today especially.

The girls would be up in a bit; Helen was letting them sleep so they'd get a little extra rest before the big day. Last night, Gloria had asked to be woken up extra early, too, to help with the baking, but Helen couldn't bring herself to do it. Gloria already did too much, and—thanks largely to her father—she was getting less and less in return.

Helen's day had started at 5:00 a.m. Even before the sun was up, she was already in the kitchen where she was slicing up fruit for pie fillings, rolling out her homemade dough for her famous flakey crust, and mixing and measuring for three different cakes. Early in the morning was the best time to bake—ovens and suns were not meant to be together.

While the pies were baking, there was plenty more to do. There was no telling who would drop by on homecoming evening. Helen generally kept an orderly home, but company demanded that she put her best foot forward. That's what her mother had taught her, and that's what she was going to do, even if George believed their home was *good enough* as is.

Just as Helen finished putting her pies and cakes out to cool, Dot Johnson came by to sit for a spell. Dot, a member of their church, had always been a good friend and neighbor, but somehow she had a sixth sense; she always knew when to drop in exactly at the moment when Helen was a floury, disheveled mess. But it didn't matter—by that point in the morning, Helen was ready for a break. Helen poured some iced tea, and the two women went to sit under her yard's big oak tree.

There were plenty of last-minute details for the pair to go over. "We can get Sister Gussie Lee to do the welcome, since Sister Lula is sick and all," said Helen as she sketched Gussie's name onto the agenda.

"That sounds real nice," Dot agreed. "I know Sister Gussie Lee will be glad for the opportunity, too."

Helen had a few other details she wanted to discuss, but before she could move on to the next item, a car pulled into the driveway.

"Who pulling into your drive like that? Ya'll owe somebody at the bank?" Dot asked.

"I don't know who it could be in that fancy car." Helen answered. She raised her brows and lifted her nose as she looked down the long driveway. "He's colored," she added.

No one in the county drove a fancy car like that, not even white folks. No one in the next county did, either.

She'd seen a flashy car or two in Montgomery, but even in the city cars like that were rare. Few people in the state could afford a car like that, and even fewer had use for one.

"Hey, cousin Helen!" the man cried as he peeked his head out of the car window.

"Doe Man, is that you?" Helen exclaimed. "Whose car have you gone off and stole?"

Doe Man chuckled an easy laugh as he got out of the car. He grabbed Helen and gave her a huge bear hug.

Doe Man was tall, slim, and dressed in a crisp white shirt and brown slacks. As if he were going out for a night on the town, his brown fedora was cocked on his head; his processed, slicked-down hair peeked out.

"Why you say I stole this car?" asked Doe Man, before he removed his handkerchief from his pocket and began wiping an imaginary smudge from the headlight. "This here car is all mine."

The pride in Doe Man's voice was as clear as the skepticism on Helen's face. Helen knew her cousin-in-law all too well: he liked to take things he shouldn't. In fact, it had only been a few years since Doe Man had fled to Chicago after stealing three of Old Man Lamar's prized bulls. Doe Man had barely escaped with his life, and Old Man Lamar had never stopped looking for him.

Any able-minded person who had a murderous white man searching for him would've had the good sense to stay out of the county completely, or—if he needed to come back—slip home quietly and blend in. But not Doe Man. He came back in a 1958 Chevy Delray, just asking for trouble. A black man in a car like that was bound to catch hell.

"I'm glad to see you, but you and all of that flash of a car will have to get on out of here," Helen said firmly. "I don't want trouble." George and Doe Man moved tight when they got around each other, and Helen didn't need her husband getting caught up in any of Doe Man's mess.

"I will, cousin. Won't be no problems," Doe Man laughed. "Just want to see my cousins. I promise, I'll be off directly."

Helen watched his eyes. They were earnest. She'd known Doe Man long enough to tell when he was merely talking good and when he was being well and true. "Alright, come on," she said, before heading toward the porch.

"George, Gloria, Linda! Come out and see who's here!" Helen called before the three sat down on the porch. So as not to be rude, Helen said, "Doe Man, you've met Dot from church before, haven't you?"

"Yes, Miss Dot, you still look as beautiful as ever," Doe Man said flatteringly.

"Boy, stop. You still can put it on, can't you?" Dot blushed.

"We don't have much time to spare," warned Helen, just before George stepped outside.

"Why, look what the storm done blew in! My first cousin," George cried as he pulled Doe Man in for a hug. "Boy, that North be treating you real good I see! That's a fine car over there."

Before Doe Man could answer, the screen door burst

open as the family came onto the porch. Linda was unusually excited, she loved unexpected company.

"Daddy, who he? Who's that man?" asked Linda eagerly as she bounced up and down. "How do you know him, Daddy?"

"Linda, this be your cousin Doe Man," George explained.

"Hey, Little Linda," Doe Man sang. "I ain't seen you since you were knee-high." Doe Man turned to Gloria. "And this must be the beautiful Gloria," he said. "You still read all them books, little girl?"

"Yes, sir," Gloria beamed. "Reading is still my favorite thing. I'm aiming to be a teacher someday."

Doe Man laughed—it was hard for him to imagine anyone wanting to teach school, but he wasn't about to discourage his cousin. Instead, he turned the conversation elsewhere. "Me and your daddy were real close when we were your age, did I ever tell you that? You wouldn't see me nowhere without seeing your daddy, too."

"I couldn't imagine Daddy bein' young," Linda giggled. Gloria couldn't help but chuckle a bit, too.

George clapped onto Doe Man's shoulder with a smile. "Let's go 'round to the back so we can catch up."

"Naw, not now. I got some business to tend to," Doe Man nodded at Helen to prove he was keeping his word. "I'm just stopping in. I'll see y'all at homecoming tomorrow."

"You ain't getting outta this town without telling me 'bout that car, cousin," George insisted. "Meet me tonight at Black Gal's. We can catch up there."

The mere mention of Black Gal's Place caused a wave

of dizziness to hit Helen. She knew who else George would get reacquainted with tonight.

✴

Black Gal's Place was packed to the rafters that Saturday night, even more so than usual. Homecoming meant that there were a good few more people in town, and they were all looking for a good time. Money was coming in from every part of her house. The liquor was flowing, Blues tunes were playing on the juke, and folks were playing cards or rolling dice wherever they could find the space. And Black Gal got a cut of it all. Plus, the ladies of the evening were working double time; the two back rooms Black Gal rented out by the hour were booked solid all night long. Black Gal only had one rule about those rooms; ladies were welcome to work, but only if they were independent. She wouldn't brook pimps hanging over her ladies, no matter how much money she stood to make.

George sat at a table by the dance floor area. He put back one shot after another as he watched couples move and sway lasciviously. Everyone on the floor was a bit wild tonight—they could wash off their sins tomorrow at the homecoming service.

George jumped up as he heard the opening bars to the next song on the jukebox. "Oh shit, now," he said to no one in particular. "That's my damn song, 'I Pity the Fool.'" He began singing along, slurred and off-key.

"Hush yo' mouth," one of the patrons hissed. "You

ain't no Bobby Blue Bland. Some of us is trying to enjoy ourselves." The woman, a visitor, was the first person to talk to George since he came in; just about every regular was well aware that he wasn't welcome here.

"Where's my woman?" George responded in his drunken haze.

"Hey, cousin," came Doe Man's voice as he emerged from the crowd. If Doe Man had looked sharp earlier, he was dressed to the nines now in a full linen suit.

Almost as if on cue, a pathway formed through the crowd, revealing Vera. She was dancing with one of her girlfriends and shaking her voluptuous behind in time with the music.

"Lord, have mercy!" Doe Man cried. "Look at that young thing."

"That my woman. She gon' be the death of me," answered George. "She won't even look at me tonight."

"You really into that girl, huh?" Doe Man winked at George. "I bet you can't even get her to dance with an ol' man like you," he teased.

"Naw, not tonight. She been making a fuss. She ain't even let me see my son this week."

"Son?" Doe Man exclaimed. "You mean you got a boy by that woman?"

"That Black Gal's daughter. You ain't seen her since she was a little thing, too young to lay hands on," George slurred. "She grown now, though, and it turns out the apple ain't fall far from the tree. You know what kind of woman she is." He threw back another shot with pride.

Stella had spotted George from the kitchen, but she hadn't been able to step away until the pork was finished roasting and the rice and beans were resting. An unattended stove in a house this packed with liquored up patrons was practically an invitation for a fire. But now Stella shot out of the kitchen and marched straight up to George.

"You got some nerve showing your face here tonight," she spat, as she shoved him good and hard. Doe Man had to catch his cousin to keep him from losing his balance. "She done tol' you… if you with Helen, you ain't with her. Or with little Michael."

George let out a stream of profanities, but before he could form anything more coherent, Stella turned to Doe Man. "If it true this man's your cousin, the best thing to do is to get his ass outta here. Now. Before Black Gal calls Two Sticks to do the removing. In case you ain't know, they call him Two Sticks 'cause he beat a man near to death with two big ol' tree branches. So jus' you imagine what he could do to that old cousin of yours."

For all his flash, Doe Man didn't want a fight, and he took Stella's warning seriously. He almost couldn't fathom the trouble his cousin had gotten himself into. Knocking up Black Gal's daughter and not keeping her right might be almost as bad as getting a white woman pregnant.

Doe Man kept his eyes trained on Stella as he said, "Come on cousin, let's take ourselves out to the porch. I'll fill you in on that Delray." He kept a smile on his face and his words easy, but Stella understood Doe Man's intentions. The place was too crowded tonight to split hairs; as long as George was out of the house, she'd let it go.

Doe Man began wrestling his cousin toward the door. George cried repeatedly for Vera, hollering like an idiot. Stella watched with steely eyes as they went.

A few minutes later, Doe Man had his cousin back under control—if only because George was now too drunk to argue. They took a seat at a small table on the porch. George hung his head low as he spoke.

"I love Helen, but now days all she concerned 'bout is them girls and that church. She thinks because she went to that college she can tell me what's what. Now she want Gloria to go to college, too. What a black girl need all that education for? Not when Old Man Lamar want Gloria to help with his grandbabies. That's money in our pockets, not money flyin' out my hands for school fees."

"I ain't got much to say on college, cousin, but don't be sending Gloria over to any of the Lamar boys— Gloria's becoming a fine young gal. All three Lamar boys are married now, but that don't keep them from stepping out."

"You don't know what you talking 'bout," George said quickly. "Just 'cause Mr. Lamar tried to run you off..."

"Every man plays around George. My daddy, your daddy. Now you. Most of us ain't thick enough to step out with Black Gal's kin though—you playing with fire there."

"Vera!" George shouted suddenly as he stood up, knocking over their table. "Vera!" Doe Man tried to clap a hand over his cousin's mouth, but George shoved him away. "Vera! Vera, get out here. I need you, woman."

"Quit acting the fool George! That gal ain't got no pity for you."

"But she make me feel alive. She listen to me. She gave me a son! She the reason I—"

The porch door burst open. There Vera stood, seething with anger and practically dripping with vindictiveness. George fell to his knees, clamped himself around Vera's shapely calves, and began begging incoherently.

"George," began Vera, "if you want me, you can have me. Tomorrow. Just you wait and see."

CHAPTER 10

"A Charge to Keep" opened the services at the Shiloh Baptist Church on homecoming morning. The church was so packed that the congregation, with everyone decked out in their Sunday finest, was touching elbow-to-elbow. There were so many deacons and visiting pastors that the ushers had to bring additional seats up to the front to accommodate all the men. Pastor after pastor made his speech, each outdoing the last. Choir after choir offered their song; as soon as one choir exited the stand, the next group would file up and begin. Woman after woman caught the Holy Ghost and began jumping and shouting; a few danced in the aisles.

The church, filled well beyond capacity, had never been this hot. It was an unusually warm morning to begin with, but Alabama humidity, too, was incredibly heavy. Usually, the weeping willow trees, one on each side of the church, would catch the breeze, send it inside, and cool things down a good bit; this morning, the humidity sucked that breeze up and denied churchgoers any relief. This was fainting heat. Deacon Williams even announced that Jesus would surely forgive anyone who needed to step outside and take a dipperful of well water. Very few took him up on his offer, though; they were here in praise of the Lord, and homecoming was the most exciting service of the year.

⚜

"Mama, you need my help serving the food?" Gloria asked as she arrived at her mother's small prep table. Gloria had been off helping to sort the choir robes. She did this every Sunday, but getting the choir robes set away this week took some extra time. Every robe the church owned had been used that morning.

"Baby, I need all the help I can get." Helen wiped her brow. "I had a mind to try and catch up with some secretary work and I fell behind with the table. Lord, everybody's got their food out and ready, but here I am... our table ain't even set yet."

"I'll set the table, Mama. I'll do a good job," Linda offered eagerly. Both Helen and Gloria had been teaching Linda to keep house over the last couple of years. It wasn't that Linda couldn't learn, it was that she needed extra help learning, extra patience. She needed to ask questions. She needed things explained to her in a certain way. Anyone who said she was too stupid to learn—like the principal who'd kept her out of high school—was flat-out wrong. Gloria had often thought that when she became a teacher, she'd like to help students like her sister.

Helen was thankful for her daughter's help

and handed Linda the basket with the table settings. "Remember to mind your dress, baby," she said with a smile.

Helen had worked double-time all week to make dresses for her daughters; a cherry-red for Gloria and a sunny-yellow for Linda. The dresses were a cool summery cotton, but were adorned with an abundance of bows and pleats, and finished off with sateen trim. Unless someone went looking for a label, no one would ever know the dresses were *mama made*.

Gloria had been so grateful when she'd gotten dressed this morning that she'd come near to tears.

"Hey, Helen," said Dot as she walked up to Helen's table. "What can I help you with?"

"I think the girls and I have it covered now, thank you," Helen replied. "Looks like we had a good turnout, though. I was worried this heat would keep some folks away 'til it was time to eat. I know I felt dizzy a few times, myself."

"We done good," said Dot. "I saw you gathering up the collection money. I know Deacon Williams saw you, too. With his sticky hands and all."

"Dot stop," Helen giggled. "Deacon Williams doesn't take money from the church."

"Sister Helen, you know he been taking money. Next, you'll be saying he don't come to church drunk. I know he was off drinking with the visiting deacons this morning. I bet if you went off into those plum-woods now, you'd find him feeling real fine."

Gloria stifled a laugh. After she'd finished setting away the choir robes, she'd seen Deacon Williams, along with several others, turning up a gallon of shine in the plum bushes.

"Look, even your baby know I'm right," Dot announced. The ladies shared a good laugh. Linda, now busy setting the main table, giggled a bit too.

"That's what I like to see, pretty ladies with pretty smiles," Doe Man said as he sauntered up to the table with George in tow. Doe Man's smile was bright, and he was dressed in his best linen suit with gold cufflinks adorning his wrists. George was decked out in his Sunday best, but no one's Sunday best could match Doe Man's style.

"You do dress mighty fine," Dot stated. "What do you do up there in Chicago?

"I own my own business," Doe Man answered with pride. "See, up North it's different. White folks be different. A black man has a shot at something. I can hold a conversation with white folks up there an' I don't gotta hold my head down like ya'll do down here. I don't gotta worry about them calling me a nigger."

"Watch your language around the house of the Lord!" Helen scolded.

"My apologies, ladies, no offense intended. I'm just saying that black folks can do real good up in Chicago."

"I'd like to see Chicago sometime," Gloria chimed in. Now that she was going to be a senior in high school, even her father couldn't deny that she was old enough to speak when not spoken to—as long as she didn't overdo it. "Maybe I'll come visit you someday."

"Not till you're married," George grunted. "You need an escort, and it ain't gon' be me."

Dot turned to George. "You alright? That's the first

thing I heard you say all morning."

"It's the heat," he replied as he stared off into the distance. The thicket of wild plum bushes, where he knew the men were drinking, was only a few dozen yards away.

Helen laughed, "George ain't been in church in a long time, he just doesn't know how to behave."

"Excuse me, Dot," George said. "Helen, I'm going to speak to Henry Bibb."

"But your food is near ready," said Helen.

"I'll be back in a minute," George replied as he walked off. He needed some of that corn liquor if he were going to tolerate this heat.

George was only halfway to the plum thicket when a small child ran up to him and latched himself around his knee.

"Daddy, Daddy!" the little boy cried excitedly. "Daddy, Daddy!" he continued. Each "Daddy" got a little bit louder, a little bit easier for Helen to hear.

Caught off guard, George responded as quickly as he could; he bent down and whispered, "Hey there, little man. What you doing here?" He looked back at Helen; she was still talking to Dot and Doe Man, and was thankfully facing in the other direction. He still had time.

"Michael George, come and eat your dinner, baby. Let your daddy alone," came Vera's voice.

"I want to stay with Daddy!" cried Michael George as Vera disentangled him from his father's legs.

"Woman, what you doing here? This is homecoming. You know I'm with my family today," grunted George. "This ain't your place."

"My son's place is with his father," Vera spat. "And my place is with my son. You come 'round nights wanting me so bad… making your damn scenes… well, if you want me, George, you can have me. Me and Michael George. In daylight."

George's eyes grew wide. The sweat on his brow thickened as his heart raced. "Vera, please. Please. Helen's just over there, the girls too. Come on now, get the little man fed then be on your way. You know I'm gon' marry you someday but—"

"—Every-damn-body in this town *know* you with *me!*" Vera shouted. "Including your wife." A stone dropped in George's stomach as everyone within earshot turned to stare. Parents shooed their children into the church or covered the ears of their little ones. The old saints, the church's elders, clutched their handkerchiefs. Some folks even covered their faces in embarrassment, as if George's sin and Vera's shame were catching.

"It my bed you lie in. It my legs you between. Helen know that, but what she don't know is about your son right here."

Even the plum bushes gasped before Vera continued. "And it's time you start acting like his daddy. A real, every-single-day, daddy. Give this boy a name!" she shouted. Two deacons grabbed her as she continued to scream and cuss; she struggled against them as they dragged her off into the field. One of the church ladies scooped up Michael, who was now bawling in fear, and followed them.

George didn't know what to do with himself. His legs suddenly felt too long, his arms too short, his head unattached to is neck. He tried to speak but nothing came from his mouth. He looked across the distance to his wife and caught her eye. Even from this far away, he could see the betrayal in Helen's eyes, her hurt, her embarrassment, her fiery anger. In almost twenty years, he'd never seen her eyes so hard, so utterly filled with disgust. He fell to his knees as the crowd closed around him.

Helen held her head high as she walked slowly toward the church. She was a good Christian, not one to make a scene: no matter how humiliated or embarrassed she was, she would keep her dignity. Yet her conviction couldn't stop the weakness in her knees, the chaotic beating of her heart, or the tremble in her step. It couldn't prevent the heavy tears from spilling silently down her cheeks. She prayed the Lord's Prayer as she walked toward the church. Loudly, at the top of her lungs, belting out each line as if the words themselves were holding her up.

How was it that she hadn't known about this child? Her aunt's words echoed in her head, "Know where your husband is stepping or get stepped on." Helen thought she knew where George was stepping. She thought she'd had him under control, that someday he could still become a better man, that underneath it all he still loved her. Yet Vera had given him the one thing she never could: a son. That was no small thing; suddenly the distance George had put between them these last few years came into sharp focus.

"I'm going after Mama," Gloria said. "It ain't right for her to be alone."

"No," Dot replied swiftly, "She need this. Let her walk away on her own terms. This ain't the type of sin that should ever have seen the light of day."

As the church door slid shut behind Helen, Dot turned to the crowd and announced, "We almost as guilty as George. We thought it Christian charity to keep that boy from her. Now look what we done." The crowd murmured in response, if not agreement. "Pray for that good woman. I'll tend to her," she continued.

"You girls fix your daddy a plate, with something cold to drink," interjected Doe Man. "I'll go get him."

"Fine," said Dot. "But you best make sure your cousin comes back over here to his family, where he belong. Lord help us if he heads out after that young thing." She pointed out to the field where Vera and the baby were now surrounded by a small crowd. She turned to the twins. "Gloria, Linda, remember your commandments. Honor your father," Dot added as she set off toward the church.

Not two minutes had passed before Dot ran outside, screaming at the top of her lungs. "Call Doc Willis! Helen's not breathing."

CHAPTER 11

"That was the last time I saw my mama alive," Jackie said. "No good-bye. Nothing. Doc Willis was at homecoming, but he was so drunk he wasn't any use, if there were anything to be done. Dot said Mama was likely gone by the time she found her." Jackie's voice was flat, quiet now. There were no more tears in her to cry at the moment.

"She was the only one holding that house together. All by herself. Trying to carve out a better path for me, trying to make some kind of future for Linda. My father stopped being father to us the moment his son was born—though we didn't know why at the time. Everything hinged on Mama. She probably worked herself near to exhaustion in those last few weeks. Not that she ever let it show."

"I never knew that's how you lost your mother," Peter soothed. "So suddenly. Before you'd even reached adulthood. I don't know how you ever bore that."

"Heart attacks are quick," continued Jackie. "If there's any mercy, it's that. The church people said she died of a broken heart, the fools. Her heart gave out from the shock, pure and simple. How she ever had the strength to walk into that church, I'll never know."

"Strong women raise strong daughters," Peter replied. He again began running his hand up and down Jackie's spine, stroking away the worst of her tension.

"The funeral was a circus. Every black person in the county was there, I think. Even Black Gal showed up, although she had the good sense not to stay too long. Slipped some money to Linda to pay for the household expenses, which was a kindness, I guess, or an apology, maybe. I don't know. I'm sure Black Gal knew better than any of us just how useless my father really was. In any case, Linda gave me the money the next day, just like Black Gal instructed her to ..." Jackie trailed off for a moment, then almost smiled. "Linda, God love her, didn't really understand what was happening at the wake. She kept asking why Mama was sleeping in the parlor."

Peter tried to laugh. A pathetic, forced, half-chuckle came from his throat. Only half his mouth managed a smile.

"Everyone said what a good woman Mama was. How she kept her wedding vows. They praised her church work. Pastor Johnson kept calling her a good Christian woman. She would've liked that, I think. But I couldn't take it. I spent most of the wake in my room, hiding under the sheets like a little girl. I felt it was my fault. If I hadn't made her press my father about Montgomery Lab. If I hadn't insisted on that new dress. If I hadn't spent so many hours reading when I could've been picking up her burden. If I'd ever gotten my nose out of a book, I might've found out about the baby. I knew my father wasn't faithful—she knew it too—but if I'd known about

Michael George, I could've broke it to her gentle. There wouldn't have been a scene."

Peter looked his wife in the eyes. He knew Jackie well enough not to say anything as painfully obvious as, "It wasn't your fault," so instead he just held her gaze, letting his eyes reflect his oceans of sympathy, patience.

"Dot was real kind to us, though. She checked on us every day, made sure we were provided for those first few weeks. And the services... she and the church ladies took care of everything. She let me be alone with my grief at the wake, held the circus at bay. I'll always be grateful for that. My father's sister Mary, too, tried to do her part, even though we hadn't been close to her—she was born-again, and she and my father didn't see eye-to-eye. I almost wish she had stayed away; I could barely tolerate her 'Jesus' will' nonsense. My mother was dead at forty-two. I didn't see a damn thing divine in that."

Jackie crossed her arms on the table, curled her head into them. There was still so much more to tell. She didn't have the energy. She wasn't even sure she had the energy to get up from the table.

⚜

The water swirled around Jackie's body, enveloping her, as she let her mind go numb. Peter had insisted on drawing her a bath. He said her clenched muscles needed some time in their home's large soaking tub, said she needed the water to hold her up while she rested a bit. Jackie was so spent she hadn't objected to either of these statements. It was the first time in twenty-five years of marriage that she'd let Peter draw her a bath. He'd even added the lavender salts she found so calming.

Jackie suspected that Peter needed a break, too. That was fine. She'd just dumped the first sixteen years of her life in his lap, sixteen years of a person he never knew was a part of her. He needed a minute to take in all of it. They weren't fighting—thankfully—but her husband needed a moment to retreat into his corner. That was the least she could give him. Perhaps the *only* thing she could give him.

When Jackie awoke, Peter was at the foot of the tub carefully adding more warm water. She didn't know how long she'd been dozing. Long enough for the water to cool a bit, though. The fresh, warm water felt delicious on her toes as it poured out from the tap.

Peter looked at her and smiled softly. "You're awake," he said as he pulled her stepstool, the one she used to reach the bathroom's highest shelves, up to the side of the tub. He reached into the water and took her hand.

"Jackie," he began, "I never knew you came from a home like that, that you struggled like that. But look at this life you've built for yourself, look at *our* life, together."

Jackie turned her head away. "A life built on a lie. All those children I've taught, all the schools I've led. All those parents … children … who trusted me. A house of cards." She swiped at her tears with her free hand. "And you and me. I meant those vows, Peter. As the woman you know *and* as the person I used to be. But you deserved better from me, always did. It was to protect you, too."

"Well, that's what I still don't understand, Jackie. That's the one thing I *need* to understand." Peter's tone was still gentle, caring, but there was a firmness in it now too: this wasn't a request. "As the man you married… that's what I need to understand. We all come from where we come from—there's no shame in that. Why the lies, Jackie! Why? And what does this all this have to do with school?"

Jackie counted backwards from ten before training her gaze on her husband. "I've told you where I'm from, but I haven't told you what I've done. You don't have even half the story yet."

CHAPTER 12

Gloria had a problem. Many problems, actually, but this morning her biggest problem was the hole in the toe of her shoe. These were the only pair of good shoes she had, and school was starting in just under a week. Helen would never have let her children walk around in rags; she'd always been very particular on that point. Although her daughters' clothes were often well worn, they were always clean and neat, with repairs made skillfully. Gloria could sew some, but shoes she could do nothing about. Her eyes welled as she thought of how embarrassed her mother would be.

Since her mother had passed, Gloria's world had shrunk. She spent most of the day, every day, keeping the house and teaching Linda to do the same. She did all the family's cooking, and tended to the farm's many chickens and two cows. The weekly trips to Montgomery for Market Day were long gone; the only time Gloria left the property now was on the weekly shopping trip to the general store, or for services on Sundays if she could manage it. Her father still went to the mill each day, but as soon as evening fell, he headed straight for the bottom of a bottle. When the morning came, there'd be hell to pay if she didn't wake him up on time and have his breakfast ready.

Dot had been wonderful to Gloria and Linda, as had the other church folks. For the first two weeks, when Gloria was in the depths of her grief, the house was full of ladies coming and going, good people who brought breads, stews, casseroles, and even cakes for Linda's sweet tooth. They discreetly slipped coins here or there to save Gloria the embarrassment of charity, and they brought full, ripe vegetables and fresh-picked pole beans from their own farms and gardens. Her friend Vivian came over as much as she could, too; she let Gloria cry on her shoulder many an afternoon. But as the shock had faded, Gloria began hearing her mother's voice, "Never wear out your welcome." As soon as she was able, as soon as the shock had started to fade, she'd pushed her bleeding, broken heart way down into her stomach and started taking over the housekeeping bit by bit. She'd never realized quite how much her mother did in a single day.

School was the only thing Gloria had to look forward to. She'd waited three years to be a senior; aside from being at the top of the school, she had the privilege this year of picking most of her own classes. She would be studying literature and civics, mostly, with only one required math class. She'd filled out the school forms as soon as they were available for pick-up at the school's office, and she'd gotten George to sign them before she'd given them to Dot to bring back the next day—and she only felt a little bit guilty about her father being too drunk to know what he was signing. She'd have another two classes with Mrs. Stinson, who had promised in a letter to help Gloria apply to Alabama State. She'd said not to worry about the expense, either—there were jobs around the campus for which she would help Gloria apply.

But now there was this hole in her shoe. Her mother would be so ashamed if anyone ever saw it. Before she could help it, Gloria found herself in tears again.

"Stop," she said to herself. "You've got work to do." She pulled herself together and started preparing the family's breakfast. If she burned the eggs, she'd have to listen to her father's hollering, then soothe her scared sister's tears when he stormed out of the house. Again.

As she cooked, she heard her father pounding on the bathroom door and telling Linda to hurry up. She hated it when he snapped at Linda, but was relieved she'd been spared the trouble of waking him up. George's morning breath, heavy with whiskey, always reeked something awful.

Just as she was getting breakfast onto the table, Gloria heard a rustle in the woods beyond the house. Sometimes the neighbors used the old path back there to avoid the morning sun, so Gloria stepped outside to greet whoever it was.

"Hey, Gloria!" cried Vivian brightly as she stepped up onto the back porch. Her pink pedal pushers and soft white blouse complimented her caramel-colored skin perfectly. "How you getting on this morning?"

"Vivian! It's awful early for you to be dressed so nice.

What's the occasion?" asked Gloria.

"I'm aiming to get to Montgomery," Vivian replied. "Mr. Felder go into the city every Friday at noon and I'm hoping to catch a ride. Thought I'd stop and ask if you want to come with me, if you can get away."

"The city?" asked Gloria. "Who do you know in the city?"

Vivian blushed. That was all the answer Gloria needed. Vivian and Gloria had been friends since first grade, but since high school, Vivian had gone what Helen had called boy crazy.

"And is this boyfriend of yours going to bring us back home?" asked Gloria as she raised her eyebrow.

"He always treats me real fine," answered Vivian in mock offense. "He goes to Alabama State and everything. And yes, he has a car."

"You got yourself a college man? When did that happen?"

"About a month ago. I ain't mention it 'cause … because, you know," Vivian said as she smiled sadly. "But I thought now you're headed back to school, Eddie could tell you what it's like at Alabama State. Everyone knows you gon' go there after you graduate."

"Well…" began Gloria, looking down at her toes, "I do need me a pair of shoes. Can we go shopping too?"

"Of course! What good is it going all the way to Montgomery without a little shopping? The clothes they sell at the general store are 'bout as ugly as you can get."

Just as Vivian finished, Gloria heard her father trudge into the kitchen. "Breakfast is on the table, Daddy," she called into the house. "I'll be in directly."

Gloria held her finger to her lips, "*Shh.*" Vivian giggled quietly before stepping away from the window.

"Vivian, wait here a spell, then come on in after my Daddy leaves and have some breakfast. It's early yet. We got a good two hours before we got to get to Mr. Felder's." Vivian nodded before heading off toward the old bench in the backyard.

"Daddy, where's Gloria?" came Linda's voice as Gloria opened the kitchen door.

"I'm right here!" Gloria said cheerfully. "Did you think I disappeared... poof?" Linda laughed sweetly.

"What you doing outside?" grumbled George. "This is breakfast time. Now fetch me the aspirin from that cabinet."

Gloria set two pills next to her father, then sat down to eat. She waited until he had swallowed them down with a swig of his coffee before beginning, "Daddy, I need some money. I need to buy a few things."

What you need money for?" George asked accusatorially. You just done the shopping two days ago. An' we get plenty of milk and eggs from the farm."

"Not food, Daddy. I need me new shoes. These were my only good pair, but look!" Gloria stuck her leg out from under the table.

"Ohhh!" gasped Linda. "Daddy, Gloria got a hole in her toe. A big one, Daddy."

George glanced down reluctantly. "How you do that?"

"I didn't do it on purpose, Daddy, they just old."

"You can get some new shoes at the general store

tomorrow," George declared.

"Daddy, they don't sell shoes like these at the general store. These are school shoes, Mama bought them for us every year. Linda's going to need a new pair, too, before long. I got to go to Montgomery. My friend Vivian and I can get a ride with Mr. Felder today."

"Montgomery shoes cost," spat George.

"No Daddy, not much. Not at Mr. Brown's store. He always gave Mama two-for-one at back to school time, because we're twins. And he jus' kept on doing it after Linda left school. I expect this will be the last year, though, since I'll be graduated in the spring."

Even George couldn't argue with this logic; two pairs of good shoes for one price made too much sense to pass up.

"An' what you gon' do with your sister?" he asked.

"She'll be fine here for a spell. She can do a lot more than you think, Daddy. And I'll make her lunch before I go."

"I can do a lot more than you think, Daddy," Linda echoed.

"Naw," said George. "I'll drop her off at your Aunt Mary's. There's money on my dresser. But don't you go taking more than you need. And hurry back; we ain't imposing on my sister."

"Yes, sir," replied Gloria.

George shoveled the last of his breakfast into his mouth, then stood up from the table. "While you in town, see about getting a little toy, too. Nothing costly. A play drum or something like that."

Gloria was surprised. She couldn't remember the

last time George had asked for anything extra, except for his liquor. Puzzled, she looked up at her father and said, "Daddy, Linda doesn't need a drum, not even to play with. It's already hard enough to get her to stay focused. And you know how she hates loud noises."

Anger flared on George's face. "Who you talking to?" he spat. "Do as I say before I change my mind and don't let you have no shoes at all!"

Gloria knew she had pushed too far. "I'm sorry, Daddy." She lowered her eyes in contrition. "I was just saying that a drum wouldn't be a good idea for Linda, that's all."

"Who said I was getting it for Linda? Does everything in my life have to be about you girls?"

"Then who's it for, Daddy?"

"Never you mind. Just get it. Now tie your sister's shoes up properly and get her ready to go."

Gloria let it drop. It wasn't worth fighting about, wasn't worth making Linda cry. She looked down at her sister's shoes—she hadn't done up her laces again. Linda always forgot that part.

"Come on Linda, I'll do one, you do the other. It's a race!"

Linda bent down and grabbed her left shoe. "One ... two ... three ... GO!" she cried, before beginning to work the laces as quickly as she could.

"You won!" exclaimed Gloria. "You beat me! Now you go on and have a good day at Aunt Mary's. I'll come get you later."

❊

Gloria watched from the front porch as her father backed out of the driveway. She knew she couldn't let Vivian in until he turned down the road. As she watched the old truck drive away, she thought about the toy drum. Such a strange request.

That's when it suddenly hit her—really hit her for the first time. She had a baby brother, one that she'd never met. The toy drum was for little Michael.

CHAPTER 13

Gloria and Vivian spent a solid forty-five minutes in Mr. Felder's truck on the way into Montgomery. Mr. Felder was a nice man, talkative and friendly, but the ride seemed to take hours: both girls were eager to arrive in the city.

"Washington Park is just up this way a stretch," announced Mr. Felder as the rural landscape finally gave way to the city's paved streets and tall buildings. "Montgomery is a big city, ladies, but don't you go stepping outside of the colored district. No good can come of that," he warned.

"Don't you worry, Mr. Felder," began Vivian. "We've both been to Montgomery before, sir. We just going to Brown's Shoe Store an' maybe a couple places nearby. If we have time, we might stop in at Miss Mae's Beauty Shop and have us a look at the new nail polish colors—my mama lets me paint my nails on special occasions." Vivian added the last part quickly; Mr. Felder was old-fashioned and not likely to approve of flashy makeup.

"We'd be obliged if you could drop us at Hill Street

and Dillard, sir." Gloria said. "Mr. Brown's is right off the corner there."

"Alright then," Mr. Felder said as he pulled towards the curb. "Like I said before, I won't be headed back home 'til late. You girls will have to find your own way back."

"We got that all worked our already, sir," began Vivian. "I got my cousin Paul here in town, he'll take us back. I'm gon' go over there to that telephone booth and let him know we arrived safe. "

Mr. Felder approved. "That's mighty responsible of you, Vivian." He put his truck in park. "Ok girls. There's a lot that goes on in Washington Park. Be careful."

"We will, sir. We appreciate everything," Gloria said as she and Vivian slid out of the truck's cabin. The girls stood by the curb and waved as Mr. Felder drove away.

"First thing's first," said Gloria. "Let's get me those new shoes. I can't be seen walking around like this. Mama would roll over in her grave."

"Alright, Gloria, but we have to hurry. We suppose to meet Eddie in an hour." Vivian replied. "He hates it when I'm late."

✂

"Those are some smart shoes, Gloria," Vivian said as the girls walked out of Mr. Brown's. "But not so pretty your Daddy will start hollerin'. They catch the light real nice as you walk."

"They should last us all year, too," Gloria replied, as she held up the shopping bag that contained Linda's pair.

"We've got just enough time to meet Eddie," said Vivian. "Come on, let's hurry."

"I thought we were meeting Eddie here, in the shopping district?"

"We are... just about. It's just a couple blocks away. Around that corner on Mill Street, then three or four streets down."

Gloria kept in step with Vivian as they walked along Mill Street. The neighborhood changed quickly; the glitz and flash of the main drag turned into rundown houses with idol, unkempt men sitting on their porches. Gloria felt in the pit of her stomach that they were heading for an area where respectable young ladies oughtn't be.

Ben's Pool Hall loomed on the corner. Gloria didn't know much about pool halls, but she knew they weren't reputable establishments. "Vivian, I know we ain't going in there. Respectable women ain't supposed to be in places like that."

"In the daytime it's okay," Vivian assured her as they crossed the street. "Trust me."

As soon as they walked into the pool hall, Vivian ran straight up to a fair-skinned man and kissed him, leaving Gloria behind. Gloria had never been to a pool hall before; she marveled at the tables, the battered jukebox, and the *clack-clack* of the billiard balls. But most of all, she made note of the men at the bar. It was barely two o'clock, yet some of the men were already intoxicated. She imagined this is what Black Gal's Place must look like, only bigger.

"Hey there, pretty lady," came the voice of a man

who was watching one of the games being played. His beard was uncombed and he smelled of beer.

"Huh? I'm sorry. What did you say?" Gloria said as she snapped herself out of her haze.

"My name's Willie. Can I get you a drink?"

"No, sir. I'm fine. I'm with my friend. And I don't drink."

"Sir? You ain't got to call me 'sir,' baby. Look now, your friend is over there with her man. So why don't you let me be your man? My name Willie Rogers. Nice to meet you."

"Nice to meet you," Gloria replied automatically, "but I'm here with my friend." For good measure, she firmly added, "An' I ain't looking for no other company," before walking away.

Gloria crossed the pool hall quickly, to a table on the far side of the room where Vivian and Eddie were watching two men playing eight-ball. "Vivian, you left me! I don't know nothing about these places."

"Sorry Gloria, I just had to come over and greet my man! But don't you worry, the place looks rougher than it is. You're okay here."

"That old man over there hit on me. That's not okay! He's old enough to be my daddy, and then some."

"Don't worry, he does that to all the girls. Don't pay him no mind. I want you to meet my man, Eddie."

"Sweet Eddie is what they call me," Eddie began smoothly as he took Gloria's hand and kissed it. "I see all the pretty girls are from your town."

Gloria ignored the part about pretty girls because she knew better than to believe it. Boys like Eddie only wanted one thing and she knew it. "Poor Vivian," she thought. "Hanging on that man like he's the Messiah himself." But when she spoke aloud, her words didn't match her thoughts. "Nice to meet you, Eddie." She forced herself to smile a little.

"Hey, I got someone you can meet," said Eddie. "My roommate Richard's right there, playing. Looks like he jus' finishing up his game, too."

"He's pretty good," Vivian added, as she watched Richard sink one of the few remaining balls into a corner pocket.

"Yes, he is," agreed Eddie. "Most folks look at those glasses of his and think he can't play. But he gets them one-by-one, every time."

"So you introducing me to a hustler?" Gloria said flatly. The day was suddenly not going at all how she'd thought.

"No, he not like that. He hates playing for money. He just got to do it this one time."

Gloria looked at Eddie as if he were lying though his teeth. "Well, why's he got to?"

"Our rent is due an' things is a bit tight," explained Eddie. "Either he make a little money this way, or we ain't gon' be able to eat this week… or take pretty ladies like y'all out anywhere." Eddie flashed Gloria a toothy smile and winked.

Gloria was about to reply that she and Vivian needed to be getting home soon, but just then Eddie jumped up and headed to the pool table.

"Ha! My boy Richard beat you. Time to pay up, old man."

The man who Richard had been playing pulled out

his money slowly and put it on the table. "Next time, college boy." the old man said.

"Nice playing you, sir." Richard held out his hand to the man, but Eddie jumped between them, snatched up the money, and began counting it.

"Ooh-wee! We did good today. We need to be making this easy money every day."

"Naw, I need to be focused on my studies," replied Richard. I tol' you, I was only going to do this one time, just to get us on solid footing before the fall semester. I didn't think staying the summer would cost so much."

"Never mind that. Come meet these lovely ladies. This here is my girl, Vivian, and her friend, Gloria."

Richard introduced himself politely to both women, but he smiled just a bit more warmly toward Gloria.

"Is this your first time in Montgomery?" asked Richard, as Eddie and Vivian walked off to the bar. "I never set foot in Montgomery myself until I started school last year. I was born and bred in Macon, Georgia." Richard could sense that Gloria wasn't quite at home and wanted to put her at ease.

"No, I've been to the city often enough," Gloria answered, "but this is the first time I've been in a pool hall. Is this really what you like to do with your time?"

"I do like the game," Richard replied, "but I don't like playing for money. I'd rather play at the rec hall back at school, friendly games. When I'm not studying, that is."

"You're at Alabama State, too?" asked Gloria. "What are you studying?"

"Right now my major is English lit., but I'm hoping to switch to pre-law soon. I'll be a sophomore come next week. I stayed the summer to take a pre-law class."

"Books," Gloria said. "Most boys I know don't like to read. That's rare."

"The way I see it," Richard began, "Reading tells you things, takes you places. And if I'm going to be a good lawyer someday, I need to know as much about this world as I can."Richard and Gloria went on talking for some time. Richard hadn't been kidding—he knew all of Gloria's favorite books and authors, and he was the only person Gloria had ever met who knew anything about the history of the Harlem Renaissance up in New York City. She was impressed.

After he and Vivian finished their drinks, Eddie walked over and broke into their conversation. "Hey Richard, how 'bout you take Gloria someplace for a while? Vivian and I need some time alone."

"I don't know about that," Gloria said. "Vivian and I gotta go. I promised my Daddy we'd be back directly after our shopping." Gloria held up the bag from Brown's Shoe Store to drive her point home.

"Aw, Gloria, don't be a wet blanket," cried Vivian as she walked over to the group. "Eddie and I want some time together, and Richard will take good care of you."

"And jus' where you gon' go?" snapped Gloria. She pulled Vivian in close and hissed under her breath, "Your mama taught you better than to go to a man's apartment alone."

Vivian giggled. "You're so old-fashioned, Gloria," she

said loudly enough for the men to hear. Then she pulled Gloria in even closer and whispered, "They got rooms for rent upstairs."

Gloria gasped, blushing deeply. What was her friend thinking? Vivian had always had a wild streak, but Gloria never imagined that she'd do something so … unseemly. Especially with a smooth-talking guy like Eddie. "I don't want to know nothing about that," Gloria announced firmly.

Seeing Gloria's disgust, Richard jumped in quickly. "Gloria," he began humbly, "let me invite you to a late lunch. There's a lunch counter back on the main strip— they make the best milkshakes in town." He held his arm out to her to show his intentions were gentlemanly.

"An' we'll come get you by-and-by. Then Richard and I will drive you home," Eddie encouraged.

Gloria looked Eddie up and down sharply, but it was Richard she replied to. "Richard, it would be my pleasure."

�֎

Gloria had a very good time that afternoon. Richard had brought her straight to the diner, where they spent the entire afternoon talking. He told her all about Alabama State, and the more he talked, the more Gloria realized how much she wanted the excitement of college life and its devotion to learning for herself. With just one more year of high school and Mrs. Stinson's help, she was sure she'd be off to college in no time.

It was only when the sunlight of the evening began

its slant toward dusk that Gloria and Richard realized they had spent several hours talking.

"Heavens!" cried Gloria, jumping up. "I shoulda had dinner on the table for Daddy already!" She cried. "And Linda… I forgot to pick her up!"

"I'm… sorry Gloria. I didn't give one lick of thought to the time, either," said Richard. "Where are Eddie and Vivian? They ought to have met us a long time ago."

"I don't know, but I've got to get home. I wouldn't put it past my daddy to give me a whipping for this." Gloria blushed as she realized she'd just admitted that George still whipped her like a child.

"I'll make this right," Richard said. "I'm going back to the pool hall to get them. And if they won't come, I'll get Eddie's car keys and drive you home myself." He paused for a moment and looked around the diner, which was now filling up with dinnertime guests. "Will you be alright here by yourself for a spell?" he asked gently.

"Better here than that pool hall, thank you."

"Miss… Miss?" Richard called to the waitress. "This here is for a slice of pie for the young lady, and for a magazine of her choice from the rack over there. I'll be back for her directly," he said as he slid some money onto their table. He turned back to Gloria. "I'll be as quick as I can. You just set here and read in the meantime. This place is open late, till 8:00 p.m., but I'll be back well before that."

Despite the worry that had taken over her body, Gloria relaxed into Richard's kindness. "Thank you. I'll be fine. I trust you."

✂

Twenty minutes later, Gloria climbed into the backseat of Eddie's car. She exchanged a few cross words with Vivian, but thought it best to avoid too much of a fuss. Even though she trusted Richard, she made sure to put her shopping bag in between the two of them in the backseat, for respectability.

The drive home was long, longer than the ride in. Eddie's sedan wasn't made for the red clay country roads and the many potholes along the way. He had to keep switching gears, and they stalled out completely two or three times.

"How far do you stay in these woods?" asked Eddie, turning to Vivian. They'd been driving for over forty minutes now. "I thought you said you were just over the county line?" Vivian didn't know it, but Eddie was annoyed because he had another date that evening with his main girl and would now be late to pick her up.

"We almost there, not long now. Turn down this road, Route Twenty-one," instructed Vivian, sounding a bit vexed.

"I ain't trying to rush," Eddie began. "I just got to get up early to go to class and all. Ain't that right, Richard?"

Richard and Gloria had continued their conversation softly in the backseat for most of the ride. Richard wanted to take Gloria's mind off the hell she'd catch at home, and Gloria wanted to soak in every moment she could with Richard. By now, they were holding hands across the middle seat.

"Hey Richard, you listening to me? Ain't I got class in the morning?" Eddie repeated.

"I don't know what you talking about," Richard said honestly. "We're in-between terms these two weeks. Fall classes don't begin till after Labor Day. An' in any case, tomorrow is Saturday."

"Huh…" hesitated Eddie, "You know I'm taking that weekend supplemental." It was such a bald lie that even Gloria could spot it, but Vivian didn't seem to notice—or if she did, she didn't care.

Richard took Gloria's hand again and they continued their conversation. Eddie turned off the main road at Vivian's instruction. Very soon their route turned into little more than a pathway in the darkening twilight.

Richard had never met anyone quite like Gloria; here she was, little more than a month past seventeen, yet she was already better read that any college girl he'd met. He admired the way she cared for Linda, and he was certain Gloria would find ways of helping others like her sister when she finally became a teacher. Plus, they shared a common goal, too: Gloria wanted to better the Negro's world through education, just like he wanted to change it through law.

When the car came to the next intersection, Gloria said, "Stop the car Eddie. We can walk from here."

"It's not far now," added Vivian. "We can't let our daddies see us driving home with boys."

Eddie was clearly relieved that he could now head back to Montgomery, but Richard spoke up before his roommate could say as much. "Let us walk to you to your doors, ladies. It's too late for you to be out alone. The moon's already rising."

Gloria looked up and saw the full moon hanging in the later-summer sky. "Thank you kindly, but we'll be fine from here. Come on Vivian, I've got to get on home."

Before Gloria could so much as collect her parcel, Richard had jumped up, and run around the back of the car. He was now opening Gloria's door for her. He took her hand to help her out. As she stood up, she looked into his deep brown eyes, remorseful that their time together was at an end.

"I hope you won't think me too forward," Richard started shyly, "but I took the liberty of writing down my number. I'd like to take yours as well, if you'll allow it. I'd like to see you again. I can show you the campus."

"I'd like that," Gloria replied, "but I don't have a telephone. I can use the pay phone at the general store, though. I'll be doing the regular shopping on Wednesday afternoons, after school."

Gloria turned, expecting to see Vivian getting out of the car. Instead, her friend was busy kissing Eddie. Passionately. Gloria took a small step back from the car in disgust.

"Hey Eddie, these ladies need to get home," called Richard, saving Gloria the embarrassment. Then he turned back to Gloria. "Don't worry, I know carrying on like that isn't for you, but ...."

Before she realized what he was doing, Richard swiftly planted a soft kiss on her cheek. Gloria's insides turned to honey. She laughed despite herself, then gave Richard a big hug in return.

Just as their embrace ended, Vivian grabbed Gloria by the hand as if she were suddenly in a big hurry. "Time to go. Let's get moving."

The four said their goodbyes. Richard climbed into the front seat and the car started back down the country road, bumping all the way. Vivian and Gloria waved until Eddie's taillights became red dots in the distance.

"You like Richard a lot, Gloria, don't you?"

"You know I do. An' I ain't even worried about being in trouble. I know my daddy's gon' have a fit, 'specially since he had to pick up Linda himself. But to be honest, it was worth it."

The girls walked together in the dark until they came to the intersection leading to Gloria's house.

"Good luck, Gloria. Don't let your daddy holler too much. I'll see you when school starts on Wednesday," said Vivian.

"Yes, see you then. Get yourself on home, and good luck sneaking in!"

As Gloria turned onto the little road that led to her house, her mind jumped from rapture to worry. Lying to her parents was something she did not do. Other than omitting a fact here or there to keep her daddy calm, she couldn't remember ever intentionally lying to him. Yet, at the same time, the truth was out of the question.

Gloria paused for a moment, considering how to handle this. Then she lifted her chin bravely and resolved to do the best she could. Her daddy could scream all he wanted: this was the first time she'd felt human, hopeful and light, since her mama had passed. School was less than a week away, with college—and maybe Richard—to follow.

CHAPTER 14

"Where the hell you been?" George snapped as Gloria walked into the front room. Her Aunt Mary stood just behind him, sucking her teeth and scowling.

"I tol' you, Daddy, I went into Montgomery to buy us some shoes." She held out her shopping bag like a shield. "Two-for-one at Mr. Brown's, remember?"

"It's nine o'clock at night!" shouted Mary. "You weren't doing no shopping at 9:00 p.m.! Every store in Montgomery is closed by six in the evening, an' I know that for a fact. Now where have you been, girl?"

"I jus' said… I was in Montgomery. I missed my ride home with Mr. Felder."

"Mr. Felder?" Mary asked accusatorily. "What you waiting on Mr. Felder for?"

"He took Vivian and me into the city. We were supposed to get a ride back with him, but we couldn't find him, and—"

"Don't you be telling me tales, child!" shouted George, as her grabbed Gloria by the shoulders and shook her. "Me, Mr. Felder, Vivian's daddy, an' half this town been out looking for you for hours."

"God ain't pleased with you for lying to your daddy and me," spat Mary. "Now tell the truth, who brought you home?"

"A friend of Vivian's," said Gloria meekly, keeping her head down. Her daddy could shake her until her insides rattled, and Mary could claim the Lord's judgment all she wanted, but Gloria had resolved not to cry.

"No doubt some city boy," shot George. "Just what did you give him to take you home?"

"Give him, Daddy? I didn't give him anything, not a penny. In fact, his friend bought me this magazine," Gloria answered earnestly as she began to reach into her shopping bag.

The back of George's hand collided with Gloria's cheek before she even saw him move. "Don't you be smart with me! What you give him? No boy gon' drive you all the way back here without getting something for himself."

The pain in Gloria's left cheek was nothing compared to the sting of her father's implication. "I don't do that, Daddy! I promise. Richard ain't put his hands on me. He's a gentleman!" One hot tear escaped from her eye and rolled down her now-swelling cheek.

Mary jumped in before George could strike his daughter again. "And your poor sister. You scared her, leaving her all day with me like that. She thought you weren't coming back, like your mama."

"I'm sorry Aunt Mary. I didn't intend to be away for so long! I always take care of Linda, but I knew she'd be safe with you." Gloria paused, thinking about her mother, thinking about how alone her twin must've felt. "Where's Linda now?"

"Back there in your room. Probably cried herself to sleep by now," answered Mary. "I ain't her babysitter. I was expecting to watch her for a couple of hours, that's all—not the whole day. I got things to do."

"I don't care what your excuse is," boomed George, "Linda don't need to be away from this house for that long. You know how she is."

"Even Mama would leave her alone for a spell sometimes," Gloria countered. "She needs extra help, but she's not a baby. I'll go see to her now."

George grunted. "You'll do no such thing. You and me got—"

"—Gloria!" came Linda's groggy, but elated, voice. "You home! You came home." Linda ran down the narrow hall in her nightdress and bare feet, then practically tacked Gloria in a bear hug.

"Of course I came home," Gloria said gently into Linda's matted braid. "And I brought you a surprise."

"Linda, go get yourself back into bed," ordered Mary. "Your Daddy and I need to talk to your sister."

"I want to stay with Gloria," Linda replied firmly. It wasn't like her to talk back; Gloria realized with a rush of stabbing guilt just how painfully Linda had missed her.

George growled audibly. Not one woman in this house ever listened to a word he said.

"It's okay, Linda, Daddy and I are just talking," Gloria soothed. "If I give you your surprise, will you take it over there and sit quietly?" Gloria felt a little bit ashamed at her words; with Linda in the room, her daddy was less likely to hit her again.

Linda's eyes lit up in an excited. Gloria reached into her shopping bag and fished around until her hand grabbed onto the handle of a wooden paddleball board.

"Here you go!" Gloria said, as she began bouncing the ball against the board. "You have to count how many strokes you can make without missing. Go practice, then you an' me will have a contest tomorrow."

"Just where in the hell did you get that?" George snapped.

"Oohh, a game. Thank you!" Linda snatched the paddleboard and, as promised, took a seat by the far window.

"At Mr. Brown's, Daddy. He was giving them away to anyone who bought back-to-school shoes." Gloria reached into the bag again. "And I got a second one, too. Mr. Brown didn't have no toy drums, but I thought this would do… it only cost but a few cents. It's good for a boy, too."

Mary clicked her tongue as she gave the paddleboard a dirty look. She frowned on toys; now that she was born-again, playtime was rightly praying time.

George snatched the paddleboard and threw it roughly onto the side table. "You think you so smart. You think your head be filled with more than the rest of us got! You think a girl like you is college material when you ain't even got the smarts to get yourself into the city and back."

"Aunt Mary is gon' send her son to college, and my

grades are twice as good as his. You know I make honor roll every term, Daddy."

"You leave my son out of it," Mary snapped. "It's different for boys. Men need book learning to get that good pay. Women tend to hearth and home, like it say in the Good Book."

"Nothing in the Bible says I can't be a teacher," Gloria shot back defiantly, forgetting her tone in her anger.

"No, but I do!" hollered George. "And I'm the one who counts in this house! Stop filling your head with those damn dreams."

"I ain't got but a year of school left, Daddy. And—"

"And nothing!" boomed George. "You ain't got NO school left. I had my hours at the mill cut today, which you would know if you was in this house properly. I only got half a paycheck coming now, and that means you gon' get a job."

"No Daddy!" gasped Gloria. "*Please* no. I'm sorry for being late. All I need is jus' one more year."

"Old Man Lamar asked again yesterday if you could keep watch over his grandbabies. Joe Lamar and his wife need help. Good money for a maid. More than the likes of you deserve."

Gloria doubled over, gulping in air desperately. "No Daddy! I'll work after school, every weekend too. *Please*. I only got one more year. That's plenty of time for you to find another job." Gloria dropped to her knees. "We can get by 'til the spring. Then I'll find my own way to college. Daddy, listen to me, please!"

"Tomorrow morning, first thing, we gon' go over to Joe Lamar's and accept," George pronounced. "With a smile on your face for the white man. It's time you learned your place in this world."

✄

Gloria lay sobbing on the floor of the front room long after her Daddy had stormed out. Aunt Mary, too, was gone, and Gloria was glad of it. She couldn't stand the sight of either of them. Gloria felt as though her father had reached inside her heart and mind and snatched out every aspiration she'd ever had. She desperately wanted her mother back—her mother, who had always believed in her, who knew she could become a teacher.

Now that it was quiet, Linda had stopped crying. She padded over to her sister and crouched down beside her, holding her. "Don't worry, Gloria," Linda whispered. "If Daddy say you got to work, I'll go too. We'll be together."

CHAPTER 15

The chickens scrambled and clucked as Gloria scattered their morning feed across the coop. Most of the chickens were scrawnier than they ought to have been—the birds had multiplied by a good number since the family had stopped selling them at the market. There was barely enough grains to keep them all fed.

Gloria collected the day's eggs before heading back into the house. She set the water on to boil for coffee, then headed toward her room where Linda was still asleep.

"Get up, Linda, it's morning. Time to go to work."

Mo'Gloree, Linda replied groggily as she stretched her arms wide. Gloria wasn't sure when Linda's special *mo'mama* had morphed into *mo'Gloree*, but Gloria was sure she looked forward to hearing it every morning much in the same way her mama had.

"Can't I sleep just a little longer?" Linda asked. "I'm still tired."

"No," Gloria answered gently. "I already let you sleep well past the hour, but it's time to get up. Now get yourself washed and come eat your breakfast. An' be sure not to wake Daddy."

Linda recited the newest house rule. "We got to be gone before Daddy wakes up."

"Yes, that's right. So you best get a move on!" Gloria replied as brightly as she could before she started back toward the kitchen. It was getting harder and harder for Gloria to hold any trace of happiness in her voice, even for Linda's sake.

There were still plenty of chores to be done before they left for the day, so Gloria saw to those while Linda readied herself. After breakfast, Linda would do the sweeping and scrub the breakfast dishes while Gloria washed up and got into her uniform. Gloria always waited until the last possible moment to change into her blue-and-white maid's outfit: she hated the damn thing.

The only good thing about working for the Lamars was that Gloria could sometimes sneak a phone call to Richard. Montgomery was a toll call, but Mr. Lamar called the city so often that it didn't matter. She was careful to only call Richard on Wednesdays, around the time when she should have been getting out of school. Talking to him was the only bright spot in her life, but she didn't want Richard to know how drastically her world had changed. She didn't want him to know of the sin that had found her now that she had to work for Mr. Lamar.

In fact, Gloria loved talking to Richard so much that she'd prayed on whether or not it was right to lie to him in this way, whether or not it was worth the risk of calling. The Lord had told her she'd be forgiven—even if Miss Virginia fired her, even if her daddy beat her. The Lord told her Richard would help, if it came to that. If only because there was no one else who would.

"Okay, Linda, are you ready to go?"

"Yup, ready," replied Linda. "I washed behind my ears and did up my shoes too." Gloria looked down; her sister's laces were indeed tied tightly. She opened the front door and ushered Linda through it.

"Gloria, look here!" called Linda from the porch.

Gloria grabbed her sweater and joined Linda outside. "What's wrong?"

"There's a paper there. Stuck to the door," reported Linda. She squinted as she read the big black letters at the top. "What does cerr-tee-ffied mail mean?" The word *certified* was new to Linda, but Gloria noted that her sister had sounded it out beautifully, just like she'd been taught.

Gloria took the notice, which was addressed to her, not George. "Certified means there's a letter or package that we need to pick up from the big post office in Montgomery. Looks like a Chicago sender. Maybe our cousin Doe Man sent us something." Gloria folded the notice and tucked it into the inside pocket she'd sewn into her uniform; she was sure to snap the pocket up tightly. "No time to think about that now, though. We've got to get moving."

The walk to the Lamars wasn't long, only thirty minutes at an easy pace. Joe and Virginia Lamar lived just over the river in the white part of town, with its asphalt roads and electric streetlights. Every morning as the girls walked, Gloria would give Linda word problems to do in her head—and to indulge Linda's curiosity, today's word problems all involved the cost of stamps. She still hoped someday her sister would have a home of her own to keep; that meant Linda would need to budget her resources and keep count of her pennies.

When the footbridge was in sight, Linda broke into a run. She loved reaching the footbridge—it meant her lesson was over for the day and she could now pick a song for the two sing. It had been like this every day, six mornings a week, for almost four months now.

Finally, the girls reached the Lamars' long driveway, where Gloria paused. "Okay Linda, let's go over the rules. First rule is?"

"Be seen but not heard," Linda answered quickly.

"That's right! Second rule?"

"Don't be alone with any menfolk, it ain't proper," Linda replied dutifully.

"Very good! Last rule?"

"If they ask me anything, call for you."

"That's right. Miss Virginia don't know how smart you really are, and we need to keep it that way. Otherwise she might not let you come to work with me."

"No!" cried Linda, "I'm staying with you. I don't want to stay home with Daddy."

"That's exactly right," Gloria soothed. "As long as the Lamars don't think you too smart, and if you follow the rules, they'll let you stay. Just do what you're told and say as little as you can." Gloria turned to start down the drive, but paused again. "But I know how smart you are, don't you forget that," she whispered into her twin's ear. "You can learn just like anyone else."

"I can learn just like anyone else," repeated Linda confidently as a smile broke across her face.

Gloria turned down the drive again. She let her carefully pasted grin fall from her face for a moment as she steeled herself for the day ahead. Another day of cleaning and washing, another day spent keeping after Miss Virginia's two spoiled toddlers—both of whom, Gloria knew, would be allowed to finish high school when the time came. But worst of all, today was yet another day where Mr. Lamar might corner her and force her into his sin.

Gloria tried not to seethe, but as each day unfolded, she couldn't help but think on what Mrs. Stinson's class was doing, what they were reading and discussing. She couldn't help but wonder what she should've been learning in her civics classes. When lunchtime would come around, she'd miss giggling with her friends. But most of all, she missed her free-study period, when she could curl up in the school's small library with a book of her choosing. Her frustration and disgust were making her sick—her stomach was often upset, she'd gained a few pounds despite the number of meals she couldn't keep down, and her body was doing some strange things that she didn't care to think about. Cleaning and cooking and submitting body and soul to white folks was so far from the life she envisioned for herself that many days she had to choke back white-hot tears of anger.

As soon as the girls reached the back door, Miss Virginia began firing off all sorts of orders.

"I've been waiting for you," she began, as if the girls hadn't arrived ten minutes early. "I'm hosting the minister and his wife for luncheon. I'm the head of the Christmas-planning committee, as you probably well know," she bragged, "and I need you to go into

Montgomery to buy a few specialty items." She shoved her list into Gloria's hand.

Gloria looked at the list for a long moment. Turned out a few items were an awful lot of things.

"Gloria, you can read can't you?" asked Miss Virginia sharply.

Gloria bit her tongue—she'd probably read more books in her lifetime than Miss Virginia ever would. "Yes, ma'am," she answered through gritted teeth. "I was jus' wondering how we'd get on into Montgomery."

"Mr. Lamar is going into the city to buy some stock from the supply store. You'll go with him."

"Yes, ma'am." Gloria turned to her sister. "Come on Linda, we're going to the city to do some shopping today."

"An' maybe we can get that letter!" Linda blurted out.

"My sister is excited, ma'am, our cousin sent us something by certified mail," Gloria quickly explained, before Miss Virginia could begin her scolding. "May we can stop at the post office, ma'am?"

"Linda needs to stay here," Miss Virginia pronounced firmly. "I've got dusting and polishing she needs to do before the minister arrives. I'll add something extra into your pay for that, but you are going into the city without her." Miss Virginia paused, scowling. "If you are quick about it, you may retrieve your letter from the post office, but do not hold Mr. Lamar up too long. If the line at the colored window is too lengthy, you are to leave immediately. Now get yourself moving. My husband is waiting for you by the carport." Apparently, this was the last word on the matter, as Miss Virginia turned squarely and walked out of the kitchen.

Gloria swallowed hard. She couldn't see any way of avoiding going into Montgomery city alone with Mr. Lamar, especially now that Linda was so excited about the letter. She sent up a silent prayer, hoping Mr. Lamar would keep himself to himself.

Gloria turned to Linda and reminded her none too gently about being seen but not heard. When Linda's face turned into a frown, Gloria promised, "I'll be back soon; it's okay."

✄

Gloria balanced Miss Virginia's many parcels awkwardly as she settled into the colored-only post office line. Gloria had managed to find every item on Miss Virginia's long list at the white grocery store. Most of the patrons there were maids in uniform, like her, but that didn't stop the few white customers from sniggering when they saw her. All the items were charged to Miss Virginia's store account, but Gloria had seen the total: the woman spent more money on this one meal than her family would spend on groceries for an entire week.

"Next!" called the teller. Gloria shuffled forward, parcels and all, and reached the window. The teller rolled his eyes when she greeted him with a polite, "Good morning," as she presented him with the certified mail certificate.

This was Gloria's first trip alone into the white part of town. She hoped it would be her last. White folks in the city were even more disdainful of her skin than the white folks at home. A deep shadow crossed her soul; if she were a teacher, she could help change things through education.

By the clock on the post office wall, Gloria only had fifteen minutes to meet Mr. Lamar. She signed for her envelope—a small but budging thing—and set out directly. She was glad that she'd be heading toward the colored part of town; Mr. Lamar would meet her at Pete's Service Station on the edge of the colored neighborhood. It was one of the few places where both whites and Negroes mingled more freely.

Fully out of breath, and with no sign of Mr. Lamar in sight, Gloria sat herself on a bench at the gas station. She pulled out her envelope and opened it. She removed the brown-paper stuffing to find a matchbox wrapped in a sheet of loose-leaf paper. Gloria read the heavy, sprawling handwriting.

Dear Cousin Gloria,

I got word your Daddy lost his hours and he's setting you to work. Sell these for the winter expenses and get yourself back in school. No way to help you with college next year, but I do believe you deserve your secondary school diploma. You should think about coming up north someday.

Respectfully yours,
Doe Man

Gloria slid open the matchbox to find her cousin's gold cufflinks inside. She burst into tears of thanksgiving and joy.

CHAPTER 16

"Girl! Get into this car," came Mr. Lamar's heavy voice. He was at the gas station's furthest pump having his tank filled.

Gloria hastily wiped her eyes, secured the matchbox in her inside snap pocket, scrambled to pick up her parcels, and crossed the few yards to the car. She loaded the groceries into the trunk, then opened the backseat door.

"No," Mr. Lamar said firmly. "You're sitting up front with me."

Gloria froze. Her stomach sank as her mind raced for an excuse, any excuse, to ride in the backseat, where it was safer. "But sir," she began, trying to hide the tremble in her voice, "what will folks think? It's not proper."

"I decide what is-and-is-not proper," Mr. Lamar barked. "You're in my employ, girl."

Gloria slid reluctantly into the front seat as Mr. Lamar eyed her with that look of his, slowly adjusting his rearview in the process. She couldn't help but notice that Mr. Lamar waited until the attendant was back in his little booth before he put the car in drive. Gloria closed her eyes and silently counted backward from ten to gather her strength.

Gloria felt the car veer right, when they ought to have turned left to reach the street. She opened her eyes in alarm. "Sir?" was all she could manage to utter.

"I'm pulling in back to check those groceries. Mrs. Lamar will be none too pleased if she has to make do without, and you Negresses can't do a damn thing right. Now give me that shopping list." He pulled into a spot between a big oak tree and the station's trash bins in a far corner of the lot.

Gloria, trembling, reached into her side pocket and retrieved Miss Virginia's list. As she handed it over, Mr. Lamar grabbed her wrist and yanked her toward him.

"Please!" she cried. "Please. I got everything on the list, I promise! Please!"

Mr. Lamar grabbed her face hard, squeezing her cheeks together and forcing her lips into a painful, unnatural pout. He held it there for a long moment, practically salivating with anticipation.

"Please, who, girl?" he snarled.

"Please... sir," Gloria began as best she could, "let go of me."

Mr. Lamar grunted in satisfaction. A deep, sick grunt. He released her face and moved his hand roughly onto her breast.

Gloria pulled back as best she could. "No, Mr. Lamar, I ain't doing this no more. I was raised in the church! Get offa me or I'll tell Miss Virginia what you been making me do!"

Mr. Lamar shoved Gloria so hard her head smashed

into the passenger side window. Before she could recover herself, he'd pinned her arm behind her back and pushed her face down into the passenger seat. She heard herself scream a muffled scream, then the sound of Mr. Lamar's belt buckle being undone.

"Don't you threaten me, girl! You think my wife gives a good goddamn about what I do with a nigger like you?"

✻

The house was completely still when George walked in from tending the fields. Farming was damn hard this time of year; even though he was only doing half-time at the mill, he still had to work the winter crops by flashlight. His arms, shoulders, and feet ached. He wanted his dinner, then the relief of his liquor. On nights like tonight, he wanted Vera, too, but she had disappeared months ago, not long after causing the scene at homecoming.

"Where the girls at?" he thought to himself as he panned the kitchen. The stove was cold and the room was just as he'd left it. He growled a growl of dissatisfaction, then his stomach did the same.

He figured Miss Virginia kept the girls late at work; he decided he'd go lie down for an hour or so and started down the long narrow hallway. A whimper came from the girls' room as he passed. He peered inside: there was Linda, crying into her pillow.

"Where's your sister?" George began, "and what are them tears for?"

At the sound of her father's voice, Linda jumped.

She took one look at George, then pulled her pillow over her head, hiding.

George sighed impatiently. It was bad enough having two girls, never mind that one of them couldn't answer a simple question.

"You know you ain't supposed to be home on your lonesome. Now where's Gloria?" he demanded as he pulled the pillow from Linda's head. "And how'd you get yourself home without her?"

"Mr. Old Man Thompson take me, Daddy," Linda replied hesitantly. "Miss Virginia made him drive me back… he lives next door."

"Why ain't Gloria bring you home? She still at the Lamars'?" Linda burst into tears again. George growled. "I ain't playing with you!" he boomed. "Where's your sister?"

"Mr. Lamar say she run off… he took her to the city, Daddy, an' when he came back he say she run off." Linda caught her breath. "But she wouldn't! She wouldn't leave me, Daddy, not like Mama?"

"No telling what she might do," George grunted. "Not with the fuss she been making 'bout missing school. Like she entitled."

Linda wasn't sure what the word *entitled* meant, but she didn't care. She wanted her mama back, and she wanted Gloria even more.

"When the last time you ate?" George asked, softening his tone. "Go on in the kitchen and make us some sandwiches for our dinner. I'll drive on over to the Lamars' and see what's what." He paused for a moment, then asked, "You can make sandwiches on your own, can't you?"

"Yes, Daddy, I can," replied Linda, drying her eyes. "I've made you lots of sandwiches for the mill."

"Well then, hurry up. I got to get off to Mr. Lamar's before it get too late."

Linda shuffled out of the room obediently. George followed her out, then went into his own room to change. He couldn't leave the Negro part of town in his work clothes, not after sunset. "If that girl so smart," he thought to himself, "she wouldn't be making me chase after her in that white neighborhood after dark." He took a shot from the flask on his dresser to calm his nerves.

George was wrapping up his sandwich for the drive when a hard, urgent knock came at the front door.

"I'll get it, Daddy," cried Linda. "Maybe it's Gloria!"

"You'll do no such thing. Gloria got her key, she ain't need to knock. I don't know who that is, but it can't be good. Now take that plate into your room and stay put 'til I call you."

"But, Daddy..."

"Move!"

George waited until Linda had disappeared into the hallway before heading for the front room. "I'm comin', I'm comin'!" he shouted when the knock came again.

Peeking outside, George opened the front door halfway. There stood a petite, middle-aged woman in a nurse's uniform.

"Sir, are you kin to Gloria Russell?" she asked without introduction.

"Yea, I'm her daddy."

"I got Gloria out in my car. I found her in Montgomery after my shift. She's hurt bad. I tried to take her to St.

Jude Hospital, but from the little she was able to say, I gathered she wanted to come home. I did what I could to bandage her up."

George pushed past the nurse and ran to the car. Gloria, with a blank, defeated look, was staring out the widow silently and trembling.

"What's happened to you? Where you been? How bad you hurt?" George asked in rapid succession. But Gloria didn't reply, even as George continued firing off questions.

"Let's get her inside," said the nurse, who had followed George to her car. "She's in shock, I'm sure of it. Like the boys in war get."

George picked up his daughter and carried her into the house. He set her down on the sofa, and the nurse covered her with an afghan that Helen had crocheted many years ago.

"Sir, my name is Easter Robinson," she began kindly. I'm a midwife in Montgomery, at the clinic for colored women. I know this is a lot to take in, so you just set yourself down and I'll explain as best I can."

For once in his life, George did as he was told. He sat himself at Gloria's feet and waited.

"I found your daughter alone and bleeding in the parking lot of Pete's Service Station. Looked like she'd be there for a good while, too. I checked her over as best I could. She's got that nasty cut on her head, and her arm is sprained hard, but nothing's broken. She been torn pretty bad, but the good news is that the baby isn't in danger."

"Baby?" asked George as he jumped to his feet. "What baby? She keep telling me she still pure!"

Gloria moaned loudly. She tried to string some words together, but all that came out was gibberish.

Easter stuttered audibly, realizing what she'd just done. She'd given Gloria's secret away... and, given Gloria's age, she wondered if Gloria herself knew what was happening to her body. In fact, now that Easter thought of it, Gloria had never mentioned a baby in her mutterings. In all her years as a midwife, she had never met a mother-to-be who wasn't concerned for the safety of her unborn baby, especially in an emergency. No, Easter decided, Gloria most certainly didn't know she was expecting.

"Yes, sir... by my reckoning, your daughter's 'bout four months along." She lowered her voice to a whisper, "Too late to do anything about."

"You ain't pregnant by one of these nappy-headed boys out there?" George snapped at Gloria. "I shoulda known better. Can't trust you to do nothing."

"Sir," began Easter in a gentle, but firm, voice. "I see young girls in a family way all the time, and it all turns out just fine in the end if folks just open up their hearts a measure. You can talk all that over with her tomorrow, but for now she needs rest. Keep her wrapped up. Only warm liquids till the morning. Let her stay here, don't move her to the bedroom. If she vomits tonight, call for the doctor immediately. I'll be glad to give her and the baby a full checkup if you bring her to the clinic next week."

George tore his eyes from Gloria. "Miss Robinson, ma'am, I appreciate you bringing my daughter all the way back to Lowndes County. But trust me, you won't be seeing her in Montgomery ever again."

CHAPTER 17

"You're one lucky girl, Gloria. You should be able to go back to work for the New Year," Doc Willis said as Gloria slid off the exam table. "Only the Lord knows why that man attacked you—and I am sorry for it—but this could've been much worse."

"Thank you sir," replied Gloria quietly. The last thing in the world she wanted to do was to go back to the Lamars', but now that she knew she had a baby coming, she didn't see any other way. Nor could she tell anyone what had really happened in that parking lot. She was sticking to her story: she'd gone to use the restroom when a man had dragged her to the back of the station.

"And do you need me to examine...?" asked Doc Willis delicately, glancing down at her womanly parts.

"No sir, your wife looked me over last week when she came to check the baby. Says I'm healed up nicely." Mrs. Willis was the midwife for half of the county. Gloria now knew that she'd be seeing Mrs. Willis a fair bit over the next few months, and she was grateful to have a woman who could examine her.

"Very good. Otherwise you're feeling well?"

"Yes, fine, thank you. Just the things your wife told me to expect, nothing more."

"Good, good glad to hear it. And what of—"

"And still no sign of my beau," Gloria answered, even before Doc Willis could ask. She lowered her voice to a whisper. "I expect he's run back to Jacksonville." She let tears well in her eyes for effect.

The tears were real, but her words were a lie. Gloria had been lying a lot lately. Telling the truth was a surefire way of getting herself strung up.

"There now, it'll all work out," offered Doc Willis gently. "You just remember to drink that extra portion of milk with your meals. You need protein for two, now."

"I am, sir, yes. But with your permission, I'll be on my way. I need to pick up Linda."

"Of course, of course. You're so good to her, Gloria. You do your mama proud that way."

Gloria had told yet one more lie. Linda was with Dot until dinnertime, and Gloria had something else she needed to do today.

�

Gloria swatted the dust from her skirt and wiped her feet well. She swallowed hard. It had taken her over an hour to get here, there was no turning back now.

She forced herself to pull open the old screen door and knock firmly on the front door. She had no idea of what to expect when it opened.

A voice boomed through the window. "Stella, I'll

see to that. You keep portioning those bottles."

The door opened halfway. Black Gal was even taller and broader than Gloria remembered, as if she were a walking wall of deep red brick.

"Good afternoon. Miss Black Gal, ma'am," Gloria began politely.

"You George's daughter, ain't you?"

"Yes, ma'am, we met at the services, when my mama went on home. I'm Gloria."

"If your daddy sent you, it's no use. I tol' him he ain't welcome here unless he sober." Black Gal made no bones about showing the contempt in her voice.

"No ma'am. Daddy don't know I'm here. I came to meet my brother, if now would be a convenient time. I brought him something."

Black Gal visibly softened, and, as she smiled, her wall of brick suddenly melted away. She opened the door wide and invited Gloria into the front room.

"How'd you get out all this way?" Black Gal asked as she motioned for Gloria to sit down.

"I hitchhiked, mostly. I was in town this afternoon, an' it was easy to find someone to bring me most of the way. I walked the rest. I've known where this place is since about the time I got to high school," Gloria explained. "Every boy in school looks forward to his first Saturday night at your establishment," she added.

Black Gal chuckled a bit. "I expect they do, but never mind that. I'll get Avery or Two Sticks to drive you back, when you ready. I expect you need to be home well before your daddy."

"Yes ma'am. Thank you kindly."

"Little Michael should be up from his nap any minute now. I'm sorry to tell you he's poorly. Child can't breathe right."

"I heard as much, in church," Gloria replied, "an' I've been praying on him. It's been on my mind, ma'am. It don't seem right having brother I never met. Even if … well … even under …."

Black Gal cut Gloria off, saving her the trouble of finding the right words. "Let's not talk too much on that, now. Babies come into this world when they come—they ain't got no say in how they get here."

"Yes, ma'am, that's what I been thinking." Gloria ran her hand across her stomach without realizing it as she spoke. "It's not right to put all that on the child, 'specially a child who's not well."

"I do my best by him, he my gran'child." Black Gal replied. "My Vera came to me by unusual circumstance, too."

"Ma'am?" Gloria didn't quite understand what Black Gal meant, but she wasn't sure it was polite to ask, either. Fortunately, she was saved from having to decide as a little cry came from the back room.

"That'll be him now, right on time," said Black Gal, rising from her chair. "Come on, honey, let's go meet your brother. It'll be good for you both to know who your folks are."

They were halfway down the hall when Black Gal whipped around suddenly. She had transformed into a brick wall again. "This meeting's on the understanding that we keep this between us."

"Oh, yes, ma'am," Gloria replied, startled and

intimidated. "No good can come of my daddy getting wind of this."

"Good," said Black Gal. Black Gal's *good* wasn't a statement, it was an order. Gloria wondered how this woman could change herself so completely in a split second's time—maybe it was part of what made her so infamous. But Gloria didn't want to think on it too much; she just wanted to meet her brother.

Little Michael lay surrounded by pillows on the full-sized bed. Black Gal, now softened again, sat down next to him and heaved him onto her lap as she cooed to him. His wheeze was audible.

"Well come on now, Gloria, set down here and introduce yourself."

Gloria did as she was instructed. Michael George was bigger than she expected; she'd barely caught a glance of him at homecoming, and he'd grown a good bit since then. "Hey there, little man, how you feeling?" She asked brightly.

Little Michael rubbed his eye in response.

"I'm your sister Gloria. Very pleased to meet you!"

Michael looked at Black Gal, confused. "Sister?" he asked, "What's that?"

Black Gal smiled. "A sister means she's your family, baby. Now say hello to Gloria. She came out all this way to meet you."

"That's right, I did!" Gloria picked up a small stuffed dog from the bed and nuzzled Michael's face with it. He smiled, coughed, and then smiled again.

"I heard you ain't feeling too good, so I brought you a present to cheer you up. Would you like to see it?"

"Yes, please… sister," wheezed Michael.

Gloria reached into her bag and pulled out the paddleball she'd bought months earlier. Gloria looked up at Black Gal as she began bouncing the ball against the paddle. "My daddy was supposed to give this to him. But if he's not welcome here when he's drinking, then I expect he's never here."

Black Gal sighed heavily, with her whole body. "I know he's your father, honey, but I can't abide that man. What he did to my Vera—I haven't had a word from her since she took off. I said I'd let George see his boy now an' again, but he never once showed up without liquor on his breath. What goes on in this house after the baby's in bed is one thing, but in the daytime I try and make this like any other home."

"I can see you take good care of him," replied Gloria. She didn't know what else to say; she couldn't find the words to defend her father, chiefly because he didn't deserve them.

"I won't even take any support from him for little Michael," added Black Gal. "Not that he ever gave much to begin with. But I don't want that man to have anything over me, or any say in how I raise this child. An' I know you're on hard times now, with your mama gone."

Michael's breathing stiffened, then turned into a hard cough. Black Gal rubbed his back vigorously. "The doctors in Montgomery give me some medicine for him. They say he'll grow out of it."

"I'll pray on it," said Gloria. She handed Michael the paddle, which he began chewing on immediately. The women laughed together. Michael wiggled himself straight into Gloria's lap, where she ran her hand through his tight little curls.

After a moment, Black Gal said, "I've got to get this little one changed and fed, an' you best be getting on home. Come on, honey, I'll walk you out."

Gloria took her brother into her arms and kissed his forehead. "I'll see you again," she whispered, then got up to follow Black Gal into the hall. Michael gurgled sweetly, which Gloria took to mean *good-bye*.

"You'll find one of the boys outside; I think that's Two Sticks I hear chopping wood 'round back," said Black Gal as they entered the front room. "Tell him I say to take you back home."

"Thank you. It's a mighty long walk from here. An' I appreciate your having me, unexpected and all." Gloria took a good look around the front room for the first time: for such a notorious place, Black Gal's looked just like any other home, except maybe a little bigger. She supposed the jukebox was a bit of an anomaly, but what harm could it do?

"An' you feel free to come back anytime, whenever you can get away. I know how good you are to Linda... plus I think Michael's sweet on you." Black Gal laughed an easy laugh before turning more somber. "An' the next time you come 'round, I'll have some of Michael's baby clothes ready for you to take back."

Gloria's head shot up in surprise. "Excuse me, ma'am, I don't believe I heard you correctly?"

"Honey, you don't live the life I've lived without picking up a thing or two. I've seen just about everything there is to see, an' I seen plenty of girls in your way. Hell, I was one of those girls, once."

Gloria blushed hard. She didn't know what to do with herself, so she looked squarely at her feet.

"You're due 'round July?"

"June," whimpered Gloria, still looking at her feet.

Black Gal lowered her voice. "And—correct me if I'm wrong, honey—but I expect you had little say as to how this child came to be in your belly?"

"I can't talk about it," whispered Gloria, gritting her teeth. "It's not safe." A heavy tear rolled down her cheek, which she wiped away as quickly as she could.

Black Gal brought her hand to Gloria's chin, gently lifting her face. "Now don't you worry about a thing. You ain't the first—and Lord knows you won't be the last—but we can always make a way. I've helped plenty of girls like you. An' I know a good bit more than you might expect about that home of yours, too, and I think it's a damn shame your daddy pulled you out of school like that. If ever you have need, you know where I am. We family now, with little Michael 'bout to be an uncle. It ain't up for debate: If you have need, you come find me."

CHAPTER 18

Sunday was the only day of the week when Gloria could sometimes find a moment to herself. The family had long stopped eating Sunday meals together—they'd adopted a habit of grazing on cold sandwiches, reheated stew, and various snacks throughout the day. Gloria liked that just fine, and Linda did too; neither of them wanted to try to have a traditional Sunday dinner with their hungover father. It also saved Gloria the day's cooking, which was a great reprieve; she did far too much cooking for the Lamars and their overstuffed children, and she no longer found any enjoyment in baking or cooking.

Today, with the weather being especially mild, Gloria had found herself a sunny spot on the porch stairs, where she was now reading a good book she'd long been trying to finish. She still tried to find a few minutes to read each night, and she still borrowed books from the general store's lending-bookcase, but mostly she fell asleep before she got past a few pages. Since meeting Richard, she'd taken up an interest in law, too, and had read every law-related book she could get. This afternoon, though, she was reading a novel by Zora Neale Hurston—a hero of hers—and she was fully immersed in a rare moment of blissful escapism. For one brief hour, she wasn't weighted by Mr. Lamar's sin, she wasn't seething about school, she wasn't worrying on Linda or fearful of father's fits, and even the baby in her stomach had calmed its fluttering. It was just her and the peace of the pages.

"Gloria?" came a familiar voice, pulling her back into the real world.

"Richard! What are you doing here?" She stared at him in surprise, as if her brain needed a minute to absorb what her eyes were telling her.

"I've been worrying on you," Richard said. "You stopped calling so sudden... I thought I'd best come and check on you." He took his hat off and held it to his chest. "I apologize if I said something to put you off."

Gloria shifted her weight forward and wrapped her cardigan around her to better hide the bulge of stomach. "No, Richard, you didn't do anything to cause offense. I'm glad to see you! Happy New Year."

"Gloria, it's the fourth of February. New Year's come and gone..."

"I know. I'm sorry I haven't called. I wanted to. But things have ... have ... changed 'round here." Richard didn't miss the quiver in her voice.

"Changed?" Richard asked. "Is Linda okay?"

"Oh yes, she's just fine, thank you. She's at our neighbor's practicing her knitting. She's getting pretty good at it, too."

"May I?" asked Richard, pointing to a spot next to Gloria on the stairs. Gloria nodded as she wiped the step with her sleeve. Richard took a seat, keeping a respectable distance between them.

"What are you reading?" he asked. "Something for one of your lit classes?"

Gloria placed the book at her feet without answering. She took a deep breath to hide her embarrassment; there was no point in lying, especially as Richard had come all this way. "No," she muttered. "I don't go to school anymore. I do day work now."

"Day work?" exclaimed Richard. "With this being your senior year? With you smart as you are?"

"I'm sorry I didn't tell you. I ain't been in school for some time now. My daddy got his hours cut, and we can't sell crops at the market without my mama, so I gotta go to work."

Richard's eyebrows knitted tightly together. "That doesn't sound right. I know lots of girls on campus who go to classes in the daytime and work nights. Isn't there anything part-time you could do, just so you can finish school?"

"Whether there is or whether there isn't, it don't matter. My daddy won't allow it. He's set on my working. And since he's drunk more often than not now, I got to look after Linda all by myself, too." Gloria paused, reining in the tears welling in her eyes. "I have a lot to keep me busy. It's all I can do to find an hour to read."

"But it's just this one last term, that's all you got left. What if I help—"

"No," said Gloria, and Richard noticed that she seemed to shrink into herself as she spoke. "Not jus' this term. Richard, I ain't been straight with you, and I've prayed many a night hoping you'll forgive me that much. I never went back to school in September."

Richard's mouth gaped open in surprise. "But you used to call me at least twice a month, on Wednesdays after school. I don't understand."

Gloria hung her head. "I called from the Lamars'. That's where I work. I should've told you, I'm sorry. I jus'… couldn't. I wanted to, mostly, but I jus' couldn't."

Richard was silent a moment, then he sighed deeply as he reached out and took Gloria's hand. "Alright," he began. "Alright, I can understand that. I know high your ambitions are." He patted her hand lightly. "But I ain't heard from you since before Christmas. Not even a letter. What else has changed?"

Gloria retracted her had suddenly. "It'll be bad enough if Daddy sees you here, but if he catches us holding hands—"

"I want to have a word with your father," said Richard quickly, cutting her off. "Gloria, I have to admit I didn't just come on out here to check on you. I've been thinking about it, and I'd like for you to be my girl. Would you wear my pin?" He opened his hand and revealed his fraternity emblem.

Gloria's heart jumped; she smiled before she could stop herself, but just as suddenly, the weight of her life dropped fully onto her. "I would, yes, but I have to tell you… that is to say… Richard, it's—"

"It's wonderful, that's what it is! You being my girl!" He jumped up jubilantly. "I'll go talk to you father right now. I've got to make my intentions known." With that, Richard knocked loudly on the front door. "Mr. Russell,

Mr. Russell!" he called into the open window.

"Richard, please, you don't have to do this," Gloria pled. "There's something you should—"

"What's all this hollering?" boomed George as he whipped open the door. "Sunday my only day to get any rest." Then, as he took in the sight of Richard, he added, "Who the hell are you? Pounding on my door like that, making a ruckus."

"Excuse me for disturbing you, sir. I'd like to have a word with you about Gloria. My name is Richard."

George took a swig from his flask as he stepped back from the door. Richard took this as the best invitation he was likely to get and stepped inside. Gloria followed behind, knowing that whatever was about to happen next was now beyond her control. She resisted the urge to run screaming from her own home.

"This some friend of yours, Gloria?"

"Yes, Daddy. He gave me a ride home from Montgomery that one time."

"That's right, sir. I do regret that delay, but I did get her home safe and sound."

"An' I suppose," George snarled, ignoring Richard's words, "this the one who knocked you up?"

Richard jumped back in shock. "Knocked up? Gloria's not like that! I don't—"

"Daddy, no!" cried Gloria. "I tol' you, he ain't never touched me. Not that night, not ever."

"No, sir, not me!" declared Richard. "That's for married folks, I was raised AME! We respect our young women."

"This here daughter of mine is spoiled," spat George,

"and I ain't see no other Negroes coming round after her." The fire in George's eyes burned into Richard.

"He ain't even know 'til you just said, Daddy! I was just about to tell him! He never laid a hand on me. He's a gentleman, a college man."

"It's true, sir, this is the first I've heard. I just came out to Lowndes County this afternoon to pay Gloria my respects. But perhaps I should have written first." Richard looked at Gloria, eyeing her stomach. He could hardly believe what he saw; the swelling of her belly was undeniable, now that he was looking.

Gloria grabbed her cardigan, pulling it around her midsection in embarrassment. "Richard, Richard, please listen." She choked on her tears as she spoke, terrified. There's so much I couldn't tell you. I'm sorry." Then she forced herself to push past her shame and looked up into his eyes. "Please, Richard, I didn't betray you. I wouldn't, I couldn't. This baby ... this baby is ... I think you call it, *duress per minas.*"

"Girl, stop with that gibberish!" yelled George. "You think you so smart. What's that mean, anyhow?"

"If I'm hearing her correctly, sir," began Richard, with a deep understanding in his eyes, "it means Gloria and I have a lot we need to talk about." *Duress per minas* was a Latin legal term meaning, "forced under threat." Gloria wasn't using it exactly right, but that didn't matter—Richard caught her meaning. Plus, he knew full well Gloria wouldn't use such a fancy phrase if she wasn't trying to say something she didn't want her father to understand.

"Talk nothing," hissed George, after he swallowed

another swig from his flask. "All she do is talk. You think I can afford another mouth to feed, college boy?"

Richard's patience was at an end. "You might try offering your daughter and ounce of kindness now and then. Some measure of compassion." He took Gloria's hand again, even as her tears utterly overcame her. "I came here with the best of intentions, but here I find your fine daughter doing day work to pay your bills, to buy your liquor! She's running this house for you, but you shame her for being smart, having ambition! What kind of man are you? What kind of father sells away his child's entire future for the bottle?"

George grabbed Richard by his shirt. "I'm gon' get my shotgun, boy. If you still in my house by the time I come back, I'm gon' to kill you right in the spot you standing in."

CHAPTER 19

"I'm gon' die!" screamed Gloria. They said there would be pain; no one told her that she'd be torn in half from the inside.

"There now," Mary said as she wiped off Gloria's brow, "it's our burden, the sin of Eve." She sat herself on the side of the bed. "But Jesus will bring you through this." Gloria shot her aunt a fierce look that said, in one glance, both "shut up" and "help me."

Whenever the pain didn't overcome her completely, Gloria switched between wanting for her mama and being grateful that Helen would never know her shame. Her mother had held such high hopes for her, nurtured her everyday of her life, yet Gloria had now been lowered to the point where most days she couldn't even think straight. This baby, who she loved despite everything, would be the end of all her dreams. The finality of it only added to each of Gloria's screams.

"You doing just fine, honey. Every new mother feels this, I promise you it's normal. And you're almost there. Two more pushes and we will have a baby," said Mrs. Willis.

With Gloria being so young, Mary had sent for the midwife as soon as news of Gloria's labor had reached her porch. George had arrived at her house in a half-drunk frenzy, without a clue about what to do. As if he hadn't seen Helen birth his twins, as if the whole concept of a baby coming into the world was new to him.

Evening was just now approaching. Gloria's labor hadn't been long, especially for a new mother. The pains had started early in the morning with the sun, but she'd kept them to herself so as not to alarm Linda. As noon approached and the pain became almost impossible to hide, Gloria had sent Linda to Dot's with instructions to "help bake a scratch cake." That was the signal she and Dot had worked out in advance—the last thing Gloria wanted was for her sister, always so sensitive, to witness the labor. Gloria's water had broken three hours later, and that's when George flew off to Mary's, leaving her alone—a frightening moment during which she prayed to the Lord desperately.

"Come on now, push Gloria," instructed Mrs. Willis again. "Almost there, almost there. The longer you wait after a contraction, the harder it is to get the baby moving again. Work with your body. Now push so you can meet your child."

"But I can't! It hurt too bad. I can't do this. I can't." But no sooner had Gloria finished, a pain so intense that her vision went black hit her. She never knew human beings had the capacity to feel so much pain.

She screamed a scream she didn't even know she was capable of. Her body had taken over, she had no choice. She pushed as if it were the last thing she'd ever do. She pushed, half-convinced that it *would* be the last thing she ever did.

"A boy! A fine young boy," announced Mrs. Willis, just as the baby drew his first breath and broke into a strong, healthy cry. She whisked the newborn over to the dresser and began washing him. All Gloria could see was the top of her son's little head.

"Give him here!" Gloria cried. "I need my baby." She wanted her son in her arms before the other two women could get a good look at him. She'd stuck to her story, but she'd very purposefully crafted her lie so as not to mention her beau's skin. She'd left that part out to protect the unborn baby, even more than herself—mixing races was dangerous.

Mary got up and walked over to the dresser to retrieve the baby. She looked down at her great-nephew, now cleaned and freshened, and gasped. "That ain't no colored baby!" she exclaimed. "This here a white baby."

"Now Mary, you know sometimes it takes a day or so for their color to take, it's natur—"

Gloria cut Mrs. Willis off. "His name is Anthony. And I never said the father was colored."

CHAPTER 20

E ven George couldn't deny Gloria her six weeks rest, but those six weeks were now up. Homecoming had come and gone during those weeks—the pastor had asked the family to stay away this year—and tomorrow would be Gloria's first day back at work. She was frightened; she could only pray that Mr. Lamar had sense enough to know that she was still healing. He hadn't touched her in her last months of pregnancy, and she hoped the same kind of taboo would keep him away from her so soon after giving birth.

For the past six weeks, George had brought Linda to the Lamars' in Gloria's place. Linda couldn't manage all a maid's duties, but she could handle the basics, plus she was very good with the children. Since the Lamars had never been able to hold a maid, Miss Virginia reluctantly let Linda do half-days with no cooking. For half-pay, of course. To keep Linda from ever getting lost along route back, Mr. Felder had been kind enough to pick her up after work each evening and drive her home. The days were long enough now to allow for that.

In that time, Richard had visited Gloria on

three afternoons, in secret of course. She knew it wasn't proper having a boy alone in the house, but she supposed—as the unwed mother to a half-white baby—her reputation was as spoiled now as it ever could be. Once she'd explained everything to Richard and trusted him will her many secrets, Richard had shown the most beautiful patience and understanding she'd ever known. When she cried, he'd held her tenderly. He'd prayed with her. They'd kissed on the lips twice, but Richard still treated her with the same chaste respect he always had. When they talked, their conversations were far more about law, literature, and improving the Negro's condition than about the state in which Gloria now lived.

If there were any blessing in going back to work, it was that Gloria was returning on a Wednesday. She wouldn't have to do a full week; it would be a good test to see where her body was. Come Saturday night, if it was too much, she supposed Linda could take over for one more week. She hated the idea of Linda working— her sister had come home cranky and unusually sullen on many an evening—but Gloria knew she had to take care of herself too, now; she had a baby depending on her.

Gloria walked into her bedroom, where Tony lay in his cradle. The clothes and other items Black Gal had packed up were invaluable; Gloria had barely needed to buy a thing for the baby. Swaddling blankets, diapers, booties, bibs, and even a few stuffed toys—Black Gal had thought of everything. To save herself the headache, Gloria had told her father that the donations had come from the church.

"There now little man," she said as she lifted her son, "Auntie Linda will be home in just a little while. Let's get you fed before she gets back." Gloria brought her son to her breast and waited for the moment when he would latch. He was getting better at latching on all by himself, and Gloria marveled daily as she watched her boy grow more and more aware of the world around him. She was grateful that the summer evening wasn't too hot; Tony always took more milk when it was cooler. She hummed to him as he suckled. She wished desperately that her mama was still alive so she could see Tony's sweetness.

Gloria had just got the baby changed and settled when she heard a loud thud on the front porch, followed by a cry of pain. She ran to the front door to see what happened.

"Linda!" Gloria cried as she sat down beside her sister on the top step. "What happened? Are you hurt?"

"Gloree, my knee!" Linda held her knee to her chest as she rocked back and forth.

Gloria examined her sister's leg. It was bleeding, but it was little more than a scrape, really. If Linda were truly injured, her knee would be swelling already.

"Well, if you want to knock your knees clean off, you're just going to have to try harder next time," Gloria chided.

Linda smiled. "Yes, I'll try harder next time."

"A touch of iodine and a bandage is all you need. Maybe some ice later if it's sore. You'll be fine," said Gloria, looking the cut over again. "Now, what happened? How'd you fall?"

"I was jus' running down the drive, an' the stairs jumped up at me."

Gloria laughed a little. "The stairs jumped up at me," was something their mother always said. Helen had a habit of stubbing her toe on the first step, especially when she was carrying bundles into the house.

"And no small wonder too, your shoes are undone again!" exclaimed Gloria. "Did you tie them this morning?"

"Gee, I don't know. I know I did the left one up good." Linda grinned sheepishly, half-embarrassed, half-kidding.

"Come on then, let's get you cleaned up." Gloria slid her arm around Linda's back and guided her to her feet.

"Oh no, Gloria, look what I done! I'm sorry! Don't be mad, don't tell Daddy. Please don't be mad, it was on accident!"

"What's wrong? It's just a scrape. It'll be—" Gloria stopped in mid-sentence; she suddenly saw why Linda was so upset. Her uniform was torn from her shoulder to the top of her stomach. The gash in the fabric was gaping; now that she was standing up, Linda's camisole was showing through.

"Oh, Linda! You must of got yourself snagged on one of them old nails as you fell. Get in the house before anyone sees your underclothes."

Gloria sat Linda down at the kitchen table, then she tiptoed her into their room to get a fresh dress for her sister. The baby was now asleep and she wanted to keep it that way. She couldn't help but smile at the sound of Tony's soft breathing.

"Okay, Linda, let's get that knee patched up and then you can get changed in Daddy's room," said Gloria, searching the cabinet for the first aid kit. Before she tended to Linda's knee, she took one more look at the uniform. "This ain't even a rip I can sew. It's across the whole front, not on the seams or anything."

"But Gloria," cried Linda, "What you gon' wear tomorrow?"

"The spare, silly."

"Gloria, this *is* the spare, remember? The other one got that big stain."

Gloria considered this. Yesterday Linda had come home with a big greasy mess across the front of the uniform's skirt. Gloria had covered the stain in a salt-paste and set it on the back porch; it would be a day or two yet before the salt would work its magic and lift the grease from the fabric as it was washed.

"Linda, I don't think you were cut out to be a maid," Gloria said wistfully as Linda winced from the iodine.

"But what you gon' wear? You can't go back without a uniform, not with the Lamars being so *mean*."

Gloria was about to scold her twin for criticizing their employer—if ever a white woman heard her talking like that, Linda could get a slap to the face. But Gloria had no words to defend the Lamars, not with Tony lying in his cradle without a father.

"Let's not worry about that now," replied Gloria. "One problem at a time, Linda, one problem at a time." She taped the cotton square tenderly onto her sister's knee.

✄

It was no use. The rip wasn't going to get sewed. No matter what she did, Gloria couldn't get the fabric to join up in any respectable way. Nor could she patch it—the rip was in too obvious of a place. She'd tried all last night, and she was having no better luck by the light of day, either. She'd have to go to work in her own clothes— she'd tell Miss Virginia that the baby weight caused her uniform to fit indecently. She'd just have to brace herself for the fit that would ensue.

Gloria put away her sewing kit, then doled out a portion of grits for herself. She didn't usually make grits in the morning, but since she'd been up so early, she thought she'd start the day with something hardy. Without a uniform, she was going to need all the strength she could get to deal with Miss Virginia.

With her stomach now full, Gloria started her day. She went into her room to wake up Linda. She wanted to let Tony sleep till the last possible moment, then feed him just before she left for the day; Tony usually didn't wake on his own accord until after eight, and as it was she was going to have to get him up an hour early. He was going to have to start on boiled milk today while she was at work; if he didn't take to it, he might not feed again until she got home.

"Linda, come on now. Good morning! I'm going back to work with you today." Gloria said as brightly, but quietly, as she could. She sat on the bed and nudged her twin on the shoulder, rocking her awake.

"Mo'Gloree," came Linda's voice. "Daytime already?"

Gloria held her finger to her lips. "*Shh.*"

Linda lowered her voice. "I'm glad you coming back today. I don't like working at the Lamars' by myself. They mean, and I missed you lots."

"I know Linda, I know. But that's behind us now—we'll be together all day again."

"Guess what I was dreaming about, Gloria."

"Linda, it's time to get moving. We gotta drop the baby at Aunt Mary's, remember. We can't leave him here with Daddy—an' he's got to be at the mill by one o'clock anyway."

"Christmas!" Linda cried softly but excitedly.

"What's that? Quit playing, Linda. I made you some grits."

"I was dreaming about Christmas. With Mama. When Daddy was still nice."

Gloria jumped up from the bed. "Christmas! Linda, you're a genius!" She forgot to keep her voice low; the baby stirred but thankfully didn't wake.

"Not me," began Linda as she sat up in bed. "God was the smart one. He sent us baby Jesus so we could have Christmas morning."

Gloria couldn't help but laugh. "No, Linda, that ain't what I mean. Miss Virginia sent me them new uniforms for Christmas, remember? Said she wanted me wearing the new fashion for the New Year. My old one must still be in the closet. I forgot all about it."

"Now maybe Miss Virginia won't fuss!"

"Go on and get yourself some breakfast. I'll find it while you eat."

Linda put on her robe and shuffled out of the room.

Gloria practically dived into the closet. She'd balled up her old uniform and thrown it in there the day after Mr. Lamar had attacked her in Montgomery. She hadn't touched it since. It wouldn't be clean, but it would do for today.

After a few minutes of searching, Gloria pulled out her uniform, which had fallen to the back of the closet. She shuddered as she remembered Mr. Lamar's weight on her, his smell, his evil. She pushed those feelings down, way down, and examined the garment. The hem was ripped out in spots, but that was an easy fix—a few stitches would hold it up well enough for the day. A blotch of crusted, dried blood clung to the back of the collar, but she was certain she could clean that up some and hide whatever stain was left under her braids. The uniform needed a good, hot, damp-cloth ironing, too; being crumpled up for these many months had set the creases deep.

"Good Lord, help me. Give me the strength to get through this day," prayed Gloria as she picked at the crusted blood with her fingernail.

She walked into the kitchen where Linda was enjoying her grits—they'd always been her favorite. Her bowl was practically empty already.

"I found it! It's going to be okay, Linda, nothing to worry about," Gloria assured her twin as she held up her uniform. "But I need your help while I fix this up. You'll go feed the chickens this morning while I give this a good ironing, won't you?"

Linda clapped—something she hadn't done since their mama passed. "If it means Miss Virginia won't yell,

I'll get to feeding them directly. An' I'll gather up the eggs, too. I won't break even one."

Gloria got to work. She ran the collar under the tap, scrubbing hard at the blood until the stain barely showed. She took care of the hem quickly, then pulled the ironing board down from the back of the kitchen door. As she smoothed the fabric across the board, she felt a lump poking up from the material. She slid her fingers into the inside pocket.

Her heart nearly stopped. Doe Man's cufflinks.

Tears streamed down her face as she set to ironing. "Lord," she prayed, "Lord, your mercy was lost on me in the midst of all this pain and darkness. Forgive me. Forgive me, and give me the presence of mind now to figure out how to best use this gift." She chanted her prayer, just like her mama used to.

"Gloria, Gloria! Why you crying?" asked Linda as she came back into the kitchen with her basket full of eggs. "I didn't break any! An' I remembered to lock the coop up good, too!"

"These ain't sad tears, Linda, these are happy tears. We going to be just fine now," she explained. She slid the cufflinks back into her uniform for safekeeping.

✄

With the baby safely at Mary's, Gloria and Linda set off for the Lamars. Gloria hated leaving her son at her aunt's house. Mary made no bones about Tony's skin—as if his lightness were his fault—but it would have to do until she could arrange something better.

"Okay Linda, you remember how to play the figures game? Five points for every right answer!"

"I don't wanna play that game this morning. I jus' want us to sing. I'm so happy you back." Linda lowered her voice and added, "Now maybe Mr. Lamar will stop punishing me."

"What was that!" asked Gloria as an icy fear shot though her. "Mr. Lamar punished you?"

Linda stopped short and hung her head low. She mumbled something Gloria couldn't make out.

"Linda, did he hurt you?"

"I ain't supposed to say," muttered Linda. "I ain't supposed to tell," she said, shuddering. "Let's jus' sing, Gloria. I didn't tell, I didn't!"

Gloria took her sister's hand and began singing "Steal Away." Doleful, yet still tinged with hope, it was the only song Gloria felt strong enough in her heart to sing. The girls sang the song over and over until they rounded the bend to the footbridge.

"Linda, it's not telling when you share a secret with me," Gloria began gently. "That's what sisters are for. And don't I always take good care of you?"

Linda nodded but didn't answer.

"Now, when Mr. Lamar punished you, tell me what he done."

Linda covered her face with her hands, hiding. "He hurt me," she whispered.

"Just once?" Gloria asked tenderly, hoping desperately that Mr. Lamar had only hit her for some minor thing.

"No. Every week since you gone. He say it's my punishment for being too stupid to do your job right." She peeked one eye out from behind her fingertips as she spoke.

"You're not stupid, Linda, never have been. Don't you listen to him. He jus' a mean ol' white man. But I need you to say what he done to you. It's not telling. It's a secret, just for us, I promise."

Linda hesitated again. "Between my legs," she answered, with a trembling in her voice. "He hurts me there."

Gloria choked back a wave of nausea. She didn't expect Mr. Lamar to have an ounce of kindness or mercy toward her, but pushing his sin on Linda's pureness and shaming her for it was a vileness so low the possibility had never even entered her mind.

"You're right Linda, you shouldn't tell. Not to anyone else. Not ever. That's a dangerous secret. Promise me, not even on accident, you won't tell." Gloria could almost see her sister's body, swollen and limp, hanging from a tree; it brought tears to her eyes.

"I promise. I don't want anyone to know. It make me feel bad inside."

Gloria took her hands away from her sister's face. "Here's what we gon' do. We go to work today, just like regular. If Mr. Lamar lays so much as a finger on you, you holler and run for me. By tomorrow, something will change. I promise you."

CHAPTER 21

J ust as she finished washing the lunchtime dishes, Gloria heard Miss Virginia call her into the dining room.

Gloria turned to her sister. "Keep to your knitting. Don't move unless I call you." She glanced at Linda's round of stitches. "What are you working on today?"

"A cap for little Tony. It hot now, but he gon' need it come autumn." Linda beamed with pride; she'd really learned to work the needles well. "I'm so glad we're back together today, Gloria."

Gloria rushed over and kissed Linda on the top of her head. "I'm glad too," she whispered. "But let me go see what Mrs. Virginia wants before she gets to hollering."

Gloria pushed open the double doors that led to the dining room. Miss Virginia had a look on her face as if she'd just eaten a sour pickle. She'd had that look all day, like Gloria's return was somehow an affront to her personal dignity.

"Yes ma'am?"

"My mother is coming to visit tomorrow, and I need you to go to our grocer for some staples. I have a UDC meeting in Montgomery this afternoon—I'll drop you at the market, but you'll need to make your own way back." Miss Virginia paused. "You do know this part of town well enough to get back, don't you?"

"Yes ma'am, I'm sure I'll manage. I'll get Linda ready to go."

"Must you do everything with that sister of yours?" shot Miss Virginia. "Linda needs to stay here with the children. Mr. Lamar is in his office and can't be disturbed," she declared, before adding boastfully, "I understand he'll be on the phone long-distance with New York."

The hairs on the back of Gloria's neck rose at the thought of leaving Linda alone in the house with Mr. Lamar. "With as much deference as she could muster, Gloria replied, "Ma'am, I'm back now. It's my job to watch the little ones."

"Your job," snapped Miss Virginia fiercely, "is to do as I say. Honestly, with everything we've done for your family, I don't think it's too much to expect Linda's help now and again. You've not been with us a year, Gloria, yet you've had two extended absences already. You're lucky we've kept you on at all!"

Gloria grimaced as she held her tongue fast. She somehow managed not to spit out that both those "absences" were caused by Mr. Lamar's doing. She also managed to keep to herself the notion that Linda had been *helping out* for weeks now—at half-pay.

"Ma'am," began Gloria with her eyes lowered, "it's not that. I'm jus' not sure Linda should be watching the children on her lonesome."

"Nonsense. She's perfectly capable of watching the

babies for an hour or two. She did it many times while you were away. All she needs to do is keep them in the nursery and play with them until you return. She's not half as slow as you make her out to be, Gloria. Perhaps you should have more faith in your sister."

Gloria's mouth opened in anger, but she again managed to bite back her words. No one on Earth had more faith in Linda than she did. No one understood her better, knew her better, loved her better. Especially not some white old crone.

"Yes ma'am, I'll get myself ready," came Gloria's response through gritted teeth.

"And you'll be quick at the market, too, in *that uniform*. Such an embarrassment on this house!" Miss Virginia turned and walked into the hallway, but then stuck her head back into the dining room. "Be ready to go in five minutes."

❇

The bundles were heavy. Gloria supposed she was a bit out of shape from having been on rest for so long. She also supposed that Miss Virginia's mother could eat like a horse—Gloria had been instructed to buy enough flour, buttermilk, and lard for a mountain's worth of biscuits.

She walked into the kitchen and began putting the items into the pantry. She wanted to call out to Linda to tell her she was back—just like she often did at home—but thought better of it. If Mr. Lamar were really on the phone long-distance, she would likely catch hell for the noise. Except for when she was serving lunch in the dining room, with Miss Virginia present, Gloria had managed to avoid Mr. Lamar all day. She wanted to keep it that way.

On her walk home, Gloria had prayed on a plan on how best to use Doe Man's cufflinks, and the Lord had provided. She went over every detail in her mind as she put the items away.

As soon as she could, she'd phone Richard and ask him to sell the cufflinks in Montgomery; she'd heard the jeweler on Clayton Street, an old German Jew who'd come over during the war as a young man, treated Negroes fairly. Gloria expected that he'd seen enough hatred and oppression in his time to look past skin color.

With the money, Gloria would take Linda and the baby to Macon, where Richard had his people. She could only trust that the folks who had raised such a fine man would be willing to point her toward lodgings, and maybe introduce her to an AME minister who could help her find steady work. Gloria even imagined she might be able to return to high school in a year or two, or at least earn her General Equivalency Diploma in night school. By going to Macon, she'd also be able to see Richard when he was home visiting.

She calculated it would be another week, maybe two, before they could leave. Gloria could see all the pieces coming together in her mind, like a great big puzzle made up of equal parts pragmatism and hope. She'd figured out how to begin packing a few necessary things in a way that George wouldn't notice. In her maid's uniform, it would be easy to buy the rail tickets to Macon from the ticketing service in the white part of town, and she'd ask Black Gal to arrange a ride to the train station in Montgomery. She knew how to explain everything to Linda in a way that would seem urgent, but not scary. She'd post a letter to Doe Man at the train station, thanking him for the cufflinks and mentioning she was headed to Cincinnati, which would throw her daddy off the trail if he ever came looking. She even calculated roughly how many weeks the money from the cufflinks would last, in the event that finding employment proved difficult.

Gloria didn't expect life in Macon to be easy, at least not at first, but it had to be better than the life she was living in now. In the meantime, she'd continue at the Lamars' to avoid raising any eyebrows, but would keep Linda safe by insisting that she stay with Mary to help with the baby during the day.

With her plan in place, Gloria's heart was light for the first time since her daddy had pulled her out of school. She said a silent prayer of thanksgiving.

And that's when she heard the gunshot.

CHAPTER 22

Gloria fought back her panic. The gunshot had almost certainly come from inside the house. A pistol, it sounded like.

Faster than she'd ever moved in her life, Gloria flew to the nursery where she hoped to find Linda. The Lamars' two toddlers were frightened and crying but otherwise seemed fine. Linda was nowhere in sight.

Gloria began throwing open every door in the Lamars' long hallway. When she got to the master bedroom, she found her sister. Her sister, lifeless and covered in her own blood.

The anguish that escaped from deep inside her was a sound no human should've been capable of making. A white-hot heat pulsed through Gloria, a rage unlike any she'd ever known.

"Get out of here you bitch!" shouted Mr. Lamar as he lunged forward. Gloria ducked and managed to grab his knee and pull it forward, causing to it to buckle. She scrambled toward Linda, who lay on the blood-soaked settee by the fireplace.

"You Satan! What you done?" Gloria pulled Linda's

skirt down, making her sister decent. "I hope you burn! This ain't no Christian home!"

Mr. Lamar stepped forward coolly as he cocked his revolver. "Two dead nigger whores in one day," he snarled. "Sisters, too—both so feisty today. You come back to work and all of a sudden your sister has a mind to vex me."

Gloria jumped back, covering her head as the gun went off. She grabbed the heavy sliver candlestick from the mantle and thrust herself forward blindly in one fluid motion. The candlestick collided with Mr. Lamar's chest. He doubled over, stunned, unable to draw his next breath. The gun went off again as he gasped; the bullet lodged itself in the floor.

Gloria lunged for the revolver, grabbing it only seconds before Mr. Lamar drew a full breath. He lunged at her again.

Gloria pulled the trigger before she could stop herself. The kickback was strong, she stumbled as the bullet tore into Mr. Lamar's knee. He fell to the floor with a scream of pain.

Gloria looked at this man, now made small by the bullet in his leg and by the gun she wielded, and ice crept across her insides. Her heart, normally so soft and full of goodness, morphed into something dark and dangerous. Gloria suddenly wasn't Gloria anymore, she was a woman wounded, enraged, and wild. She was every hurt she'd suffered at the hands of the Lamars, every pain that had touched her and her sister. No forgiveness for this monster. No mercy. No sympathy or empathy for the beast who'd lowered her, who'd taken Linda's life.

She aimed for his stomach and pulled the trigger again. "That was for Linda," she hissed, as Mr. Lamar moaned in pain. "And this," she pulled the trigger again, "is from my fatherless son." She let her arm go slack for an instant, but then aimed the revolver once more. "And this one is for me," Gloria pulled the trigger one more time, but all that came was the *click* of an empty chamber.

She dropped the gun and ran to Linda as Mr. Lamar, half-dead and soaked in his own blood, moaned weakly. She trembled as she rocked Linda back and forth and soothed desperate words of good-bye and love into her twin's ear. As she again rearranged Linda's dress, the half-knitted cap for Tony fell from Linda's pocket. Gloria snatched the cap, said a prayer for Linda's soul, and fled.

⚜

Gloria managed to reach the footbridge without being stopped. She knew the sheriff would be on his way soon, that at any moment the patrols would be out. She barely understood how the woman who'd been holding that gun was her, but that wouldn't make any difference to the law—or to the Klan, which would surely ride tonight. She asked the Lord for forgiveness as she ran, and prayed that she'd be able to snatch up little Tony and somehow make it out of the county before nightfall. What would happen after that, she had no idea.

As she began crossing the footbridge, she saw a man sitting on a bench and reading a newspaper on the far side. She knew she couldn't be seen—not by white folks or colored folks—but nor could she go back, either. She'd had the presence of mind to grab one of Miss Virginia's cardigans as she had fled, and now, despite the warmth of the afternoon, she pulled it around her more tightly to cover her bloodstained uniform. Out in the open like this, Gloria decided to slow herself to a regular pace, keep her head down, and pass by the man without so much as a "good afternoon" if she could help it. It was too early in the day for a maid to be headed home from work; if the man inquired, she'd say she'd taken ill.

"Gloria, wait!" called a voice. Richard's voice. She looked up and saw him jogging over to her.

"Richard, no. Go away. Please! You didn't see me!" cried Gloria as she broke into a run. But Richard caught up to her in a few leaping bounds and grabbed her by the arm.

"Gloria, what's happened? Shouldn't Linda be with you? Is that—blood? Are you hurt?"

At the sound of her sister's name, Gloria burst into tears again. Richard tried to hold her, but Gloria, trembling and shaking, she pushed his embrace away. There was no time for comfort now.

"Why are you here? Why do you have to be here, today, now?" Gloria cried in gasping, shuddering words.

"I hitchhiked in. My summer classes are all in the mornings, and I wanted to surprise my girl on her first day back! I got here too early, but now I'm glad I did. What can I do to help?"

"There's no helping me now, Richard. This is … it's the worst trouble I ever been in. It ain't like before.

This is dangerous trouble. The sheriff will be after me."

"Sheriff?"

"I'm going for my son, and then ... I ... I ... don't know. You need to go. Don't get yourself mixed up in this. There's a darkness in me I never knew! Go! If you love me, please, you never saw me!"

Gloria ran for all she was worth, but it was no good. Richard followed her, begging for answers to his many, many questions. Richard's chasing after her, shouting as he was, just made her even more conspicuous; Gloria slowed from a full run and explained everything as they headed frantically to her aunt's house. By the time they reached Mary's porch, Richard looked as if he were going to be sick from the shock, horror, and gore of it all. She begged once again for him to leave, apologized again and again for bringing her troubles on him.

It wasn't hard to get the baby. Gloria had imagined an onslaught of questions from her aunt—a confrontation she didn't need and time she couldn't spare. But when Richard had circled the house in surveillance, they'd learned that Mary was in the kitchen, likely cooking dinner from the smell of it. Gloria had then managed to slip into the house, tie Tony to her hip in his sling, and flee before Mary ever moved from the kitchen. Thankfully, Tony was asleep, and he had barely gurgled as she rushed him away.

Gloria and Richard retreated into the woods beyond the road. "What now?" Richard asked. "I can maybe get you to Macon and hide you for a spell, but we have to get on into Montgomery first. An' we have to get out of the county before nightfall. Any ideas?" The first sirens wailed in the distance.

Tony let out a screech as he awoke. Gloria rubbed his little back soothingly as she answered Richard slowly. "There's only one person I know who might be able to help... but this may be a hellfire that not even she can manage."

CHAPTER 23

"I hear you back there! I know that ain't no animal in them woods," shouted Black Gal. She'd been busy counting out the chickens that would need slaughtering for the weekend's crowd when she'd caught a glimpse of two shadowy figures beyond the tree line. In her mind, she thought they were probably teenagers petting in secret—every adult in the county knew she rented rooms so folks could discreetly do what came natural.

"There ain't no use hiding, I know you there!" she shouted again. "Either come on out or take your foolin' around somewhere else." Her voice boomed through the trees, every word a challenge in and of itself. Black Gal did not take kindly to strangers on her property; there was too damn much going on in her house to take chances.

The bushes rustled as Gloria stepped into the yard. Richard, holding her hand, followed just a step behind. The baby fussed a bit, but not too much.

"Child, what are you doing here?" exclaimed Black Gal as they came forward. "Avery say the sheriff's out and looking for trouble. It ain't safe."

"Yes ma'am, I know," Gloria replied quietly with her eyes downcast. "I'm the one he looking for. An' I'm sorry to bring my troubles to your door, but..." Gloria gasped, fighting back tears.

"What she means to say, ma'am, is there's nowhere else she might go. You're the only one who can help, if you're willing," explained Richard.

Black Gal sized Richard up. "I suppose," she began, "you're the law student she been telling me about?"

"Yes, this is Richard," replied Gloria. "He helped me get Tony and make my way here. You said, ma'am, to come find you if I ever had need." Gloria lifted her eyes to meet Black Gal's hard but bewildered stare. "Joe Lamar is dead, an' I'm the one who did the shooting."

The wall that was Black Gal visibly shook. "Best get yourself in the house before someone see you," she whispered. Then, far more forcefully, she demanded, "An' you best tell me everything straight, right from the beginning."

❈

Black Gal had brought Richard and Gloria into one of the back for-rent rooms. For her patrons' privacy, it was one of the few rooms in the house with a solid lock. It took some doing, but Gloria, with Richard's help, had explained everything. Richard had to tell the details of Linda's passing; Gloria had doubled over, hyperventilating in her grief, as she spoke.

Black Gal had listened to the story with some shock,

but not nearly as much as the pair had expected. Richard could see Black Gal's analytical mind working, cool and calculated, behind her eyes, almost as if this wasn't the first time deep, gory trouble had landed on her doorstep.

"An' that's how I came to be here, ma'am. I didn't know I had that evil inside me, but something came over me." Gloria said. "My sister like that, my sweet Linda! I'm the one who told her to run if Mr. Lamar touched her! Seeing her gone from me, so sudden ...." Gloria choked back another onslaught of tears. "I changed an' I hardly knew myself! But it was me who fired those shots, just the same—may the Lord forgive me."

Richard pulled Gloria closer, consoled her again. "It's not your fault, Gloria, the Lord knows that. You been tested this last year in ways He never intended, I'm sure of it."

"An' I'm sure," interrupted Black Gal, "that we need to move you, and quick. This whole county gon' be a sundown town tonight." The baby, now wiggling on the bed, cried out as if he knew already the terror the night would hold.

"Does that mean you can help her ma'am?" asked Richard. "I can get her and the baby up to Macon, if you can get us to Montgomery."

"I'm afraid Macon ain't gon' do it, son." Black Gal replied. "She gon' have to go west. Far west."

"Macon's my only chance. The only people I have is my cousin Doe Man in Chicago, but they sure to look there." At the mention of Doe Man, Gloria touched her hand to her uniform. The lump there told her the cufflinks were safe.

"I got a place for you," Black Gal replied. "But we have to get moving before the sun gets too low. An' you have to leave the baby here, for his own sake." Gloria clutched desperately toward Tony as Black Gal turned to Richard and said, "I can probably get you back to Montgomery, if we careful."

"But my baby!" Gloria cried. "I can't leave him! I can't! He got no one but me! Who will keep after him?"

"Don't you worry on that. I got Michael to look after, one more little one don't make no difference. They family anyhow."

"Gloria, go," urged Richard. "You can't tend to the baby no matter where you are, not with the sheriff out. Get yourself safe and stay there till things quiet down. I'll wait for you."

"Richard—" Gloria began, but Black Gal cut her off.

"You not understanding me right, Richard. Gloria got to go. For good. New name and everything. No two ways about it. There's three bullet holes in that white man."

Gloria and Richard gasped simultaneously. Gloria looked sick, but Richard realized Black Gal was right.

"Gloria," Richard started, holding back his own tears. "Even if the law doesn't get you… the Klan has a long memory. Anywhere in the South won't be safe."

Gloria, stunned, stared at a picture of the ocean that hung on the wall behind Richard. The water was calm and blue, and a sailboat floated placidly on the surface. She wished more than anything she could be on that sailboat—far, far away from this hurt and turmoil.

"Ain't that the truth," Black Gal agreed firmly. Then she looked straight into Gloria's eyes and said gravely,

"You know this what need to be done. One word from you and I can get things set in motion."

Gloria looked from Tony, to Richard, to her own hands. After a long, pensive moment, she conceded in a whisper, "I've got to. I don't see no other way."

"Richard, go find my man Two Sticks," directed Black Gal. "He's probably up the road a piece, patching some of them potholes. Tell him we making a *deep* run tonight—an' mind you stay out of sight!"

�֍

"It been more years than I can remember," Black Gal began, "but I been jus' about like you are now, Gloria. Not exactly the same, but jus' about… an' I'm still standing."

Gloria looked up in surprise. Black Gal's voice had changed—there was a vulnerability Gloria had never heard. Something soft and small and so very unlike the hard woman she knew Black Gal could be.

"I wasn't much older than you. I'd taken up with a man who I thought was gon' treat me good. Thought he was gon' take me out of Fort Worth and up to Memphis someday—I used to be a real fine singer, you know—to get me discovered. I think I loved singing more than you love your books!"

"But after a time, David changed. Started using that dope. Drunk more often than your daddy. An' he would beat on me, force himself on me when I tol' him to stop. That's how Vera come to me. When I found out I was expecting, David threatened to beat the baby out of me. I tried going back home, but my grandma wouldn't take me back in my condition, no matter how I begged. So I ran. And through the grace of the Lord, I found myself a preacher woman who helped girls like me disappear.

"She got me to her safe house—I can't say where— and that's where I birthed Vera. They gave me new papers—it say 'Ruth' on my driver's license now. How I came to Alabama is another story, but once I got myself set up, I decided I was gon' do something right with this den of sin—I made this ol' house a place where women can stop. Lots of women come through here over the years. Running from their husbands, running from the law, running from whatever demon's chasing 'em. When my ladies decide to stop selling their wares, some have gone that way, too, for a fresh start."

Gloria looked up at Black Gal, her head spinning. It was almost too much to take in—that there were other women like her, that Black Gal herself had started afresh, that there was a path for her right in front of her, even if it meant leaving Tony and Richard. It was both everything she could possibly hope for now, and—at the same time—a nightmare come true.

"But where will I go?" asked Gloria in a whisper. "Who are your people?"

"To Texas," answered Black Gal. "An' that's all I'll say as to where, exactly. But know this: I'm sending you to people who will help you till you can figure out what come next. They may even help you get that diploma of yours, after a time."

At the mention of a diploma, a spark in Gloria's eyes gleamed for just an instant. A fraction of an instant, but Black Gal knew Gloria's decision was now fully made.

Black Gal got up from the bed. "Honey," she began, "you take a few minutes with that baby of yours. I've a telephone call to make on your behalf."

Gloria jumped up quickly, almost like a reflex of protest, but sat back down just as swiftly. She scooped up little Tony.

"Ma'am," is that a camera just there on the dresser?" Gloria asked suddenly. "Could I take... could you, would you, send along a picture, when I'm settled?

Black Gal smiled a broad, sad, tender smile. "I can't send nothing along, except in case of extreme need. But that camera is one of them new instant-film kinds. One of the girls uses it to sell boudoir photos. Cost her a pretty penny, too—I'm the one who lent her the down payment."

Gloria held Tony up. "Please ma'am. Please. The two of us together."

"I ain't mind taking the photo, but you can't be in it, honey. No links."

Gloria nodded, propped the baby up on some pillows, then tickled his chin until he had a sweet half-smile on his face. Black Gal snapped the photo.

"There now, this'll be developed out in 'bout a minute," said Black Gal. "Take some time with your son. Feed him, say your good-byes. We got to get moving soon. I'll get together some clothes for you, too. Something of Vera's should do. You can't be seen in that bloody uniform, an' they'll be looking for maids your age."

"Wait!" cried Gloria. "Wait, I want you to take these. For the things Tony gon' need." She reached into her pocket and pulled out the matchbox with Doe Man's cufflinks. "These my cousin's," she said as she slid open the matchbox. "He sent them for me to sell, to help with the expenses."

Black Gal looked at the gold cufflinks, then closed Gloria's own fist around them gently. "You keep those, honey. To get you back on your feet, when the time comes. We got plenty here. Vera and Michael never wanted for anything, Tony won't either. You have my word on that. I'll raise him as my own."

Gloria's eyes became great round moons of relief and thanksgiving. She scooped up Tony again as her tears fell. Black Gal closed the door behind her as she slipped out into the hallway.

CHAPTER 24

Two Sticks ran into the house and called out for Black Gal much more loudly than usual.

Black Gal poked her head out of the kitchen, where she'd been wrapping up some cornbread and sandwiches for the journey. "What's that now?" she answered.

"Black Gal, ma'am," started Two Sticks, "I wouldn't advise a run tonight, deep or not. James come in from town jus' now and he say them white folks is going crazy. Say one of the Lamar boys is shot dead. Same for one of the Russell twins."

"I know all about that already, never you mind. But we make our liquor run every Thursday come hell or high-water—even the sheriff himself know that—an' that gon' be cover enough. For what I'm paying Sherriff Daniels, he and his law damn well better let me pass any time I like!"

"I don't know, ma'am. They already been to the Russell's place, roughed George up some. Rumor say he done it, but the sheriff ain't hauled him off." Two Sticks shrugged. "I'm jus' concerned, ma'am, because if I recollect, he the man Vera took up with."

"And Vera's gone and ain't coming back, so don't pay that no mind," Black Gal snapped, even as her heart was pricked afresh. She'd received a call just after Independence Day—Vera had been in a car wreck way up in Boston. She'd kept that information, and her mourning, to herself, though. Only Stella knew; Black Gal wouldn't allow herself to lean on anyone else.

Almost without missing a beat, Black Gal continued. "Deep runs come when they come, Two Sticks, we ain't got a say in that. You my head man—I'm counting on you."

"Yes ma'am."

"Go on now and get the truck ready," Black Gal ordered. "You know how to set it up. Mind she's got air enough."

"Our guest, ma'am, she one of our ladies?" Two Sticks asked. He was sweet on one of the women who sometimes sold her services in the back rooms; he would hate to see her go.

"The less you know the better, Two Sticks. But no, it ain't the gal you thinking on. Now go get that truck ready, then make yourself scarce until I call you. There's no need for you to see her. Hurry yourself now. The more daylight we got on our side, the better."

✄

Stella had come for the baby almost as soon as Gloria had finished changing into some fresh clothes. Gloria wanted Tony with her till the last possible moment, but

Stella knew it was better this way—she knew Gloria needed to focus on the dangers ahead, not all that she was leaving behind. The parting had been brutal, but Stella's fierce resolve and no-nonsense adamancy had made her the right woman to part the two. Even still, Stella's heart nearly broke as Gloria, shaking and gasping, at last released her son into Stella's arms.

Leaving Richard was little easier. He would make the run with them as far as the Montgomery county line, but he'd be riding up front in James' shirt and cap, whereas Gloria would be alone in a false-bottomed box in the truck's bed. Black Gal had allowed for a few moments for them to be alone together while she made the last of the preparations.

Gloria had returned Richard's pin, and they had cried and prayed together. They'd professed their love, but Gloria had insisted that Richard forget her as soon as he could—if he made it back to Montgomery safely, he could have a long life as a husband, father, and successful lawyer. He could still help hundreds, thousands, of colored folks as an attorney and activist. She made him swear that no part of their love for each other would stand in the way of that. When Stella had again come into the room, this time to pull Richard away, Gloria had fallen to her knees in anguish before the door closed fully behind them.

Black Gal knocked quietly, then poked her head into the room. Gloria jumped up from her knees and tried to pull herself together.

"Honey, it's time to get moving," Black Gal said firmly yet tenderly. "Trust me, now."

"I do, ma'am, I do trust you. An' all that you've done for me… I thank you for that."

Black Gal led Gloria down the long hallway. "No need to thank me, child. So long as we get you past the sheriff, I know you'll do the same for others in one way or another. Giving's always been your heart, honey, every colored person in this county know that."

As they reached the back porch, Gloria asked, "Can you tell me, ma'am, what will happen now? Not where we're going, exactly, jus'… what to expect?"

Black Gal nodded. "By my reckoning, we got just enough daylight to reach Montgomery, where we'll drop your beau. We probably gon' get stopped between here and there, though, so when that happens you jus' hold tight—don't make a peep no matter how close the law may seem. From there we go west, through Mississippi, no stops. Too dangerous for Negro travelers at night, even under the best of circumstances—I don't care what them Green Books say. Two Sticks and I will cross you into Louisiana. Good people there, they'll take you for the night. I'll turn 'round and, with any luck, get back to Lowndes Country just after daybreak. You'll have a few hours to rest tonight, then someone will collect you in the morning an' bring you the rest of the way to the shelter."

Gloria and Black Gal climbed into the truck's flatbed. "These accommodations ain't hospitable, but they the best we can do," said Black Gal as she flipped open the box's false bottom. Gloria peered inside. The compartment was both shorter and narrower than a coffin; a makeshift pillow—a change of clothes it looked like—and a small canteen were inside. Gloria shivered; she'd always hated tight spaces.

"I feel like I'm losing and gaining everything, all in the same day," sobbed Gloria as she climbed inside.

"I know, baby, I know," offered Black Gal tenderly. "But this how it got to be. Did you think on a new name for yourself?"

"Jackie," said Gloria as she lay down. "For Jacqueline Kennedy. I think she's gon' do good things for our people."

Black Gal smiled sadly. "You ready? It'll be a good number of hours, mind. You just try to rest easy an' think on what's ahead, not behind." Gloria nodded in response, and Black Gal smiled again. Then, just as she closed the lid, Black Gal whispered, "Safe travels to you, Jackie."

CHAPTER 25

Jackie woke up with a start. She looked at her alarm clock, which had apparently failed to go off. It was well after 9:00 a.m.—she should've been at school almost two hours ago.

"I called you in, don't worry," came Peter's gentle voice from his recliner. He put his book down. "Family emergency. Which I suppose this is."

Jackie looked at her husband, perplexed, before the night before came flooding back to her. Her confession, everything she'd told him. She felt the blood rushing to her face in shame as she flopped back down onto the bed.

"But my staff ... what will they think?" objected Jackie. "I haven't so much as taken a sick day in years."

"Never mind your staff. I'm your husband," Peter scoffed, slightly annoyed.

"Yes," agreed Jackie contritely.

"I had breakfast an hour ago, but I'll go fix you something now," Peter said, his gentle tone returned. "Get yourself together and come down. I've been up half the night; I think I know where we go from here."

�֎

Jackie shuffled into the kitchen in her robe and slippers. She'd washed up a bit, but couldn't find the energy to get dressed. Not with the weight of Peter waiting for her, not with her dread of hearing whatever it was he had to say.

She poured herself a cup of strong, black coffee before walking over to the stove and giving Peter his usual morning peck on the lips. He didn't seem to return the kiss. Was she imagining it, or had her husband gone cold? Did, "we go from here" really mean, "we go from here, *separately?*"

She sat herself down at the table in her usual spot. She gazed out over her rosebushes—something that always calmed her mind. Peter slid a bowl of steaming oatmeal and a warm, buttered ginger muffin onto the table before her. She relaxed a bit; Peter wouldn't go through the trouble of making her favorite breakfast if he were leaving her.

"I should've told you years ago," Jackie began, "but I don't know what charges I may be facing in Alabama. And I couldn't jeopardize working with my kids. All these years, I've done my absolute best by them. For decades, I've been trying to redeem myself by making their future far brighter than the darkness I ran from. It was better if you didn't know, Peter, for your own sake."

Peter reached across the table and took his wife's hand. "You explained enough, apologized enough, last night." He squeezed her hand supportively before releasing his grip. "What I'm interested in now is going forward. Together. But to do that, Jackie, I'm going to need a few things. For you. For us."

Jackie looked into her oatmeal. She pushed the creamy oats across her bowl, afraid to look up.

"We need to get ahead of this, Jackie. If it's not the fingerprinting, it'll be something else down the road. And who knows how many years we got left? I want to spend them with you in peace, both of us with a clear mind and conscience."

Jackie wasn't sure she remembered what a clear conscience felt like. "That sounds beautiful, honey, but I don't understand what you're asking of me."

"On Monday," Peter explained, "we're going to fly down to Montgomery. See what you're up against, exactly. I talked to Jody his morning; he thinks it's the best thing to do. He says it's not likely they'll file criminal charges against you now—any evidence is too old to make a solid case. If you say you acted in self-defense, they probably won't challenge it. You were a minor, too, and that counts for something."

"I can't go back to that life, I can't!" cried Jackie. "Just because your brother is a lawyer doesn't mean he knows what's best for us." She paused, wiping a tear from her face. "Probably leaves a lot up in the air, Peter. And I can't just leave. I have school, I have to see this year through. There's not even three more months until I retire, until my pension is secure."

"Truth told, Jackie, you got enough days saved up to retire now. And that's what you need to do. If you don't go back, you'll never be fingerprinted. You'll never run the risk of being flagged for investigation. Your legacy will be safe. Your pension will be safe. Our future will be safe."

"Not if I'm in jail, it won't be."

"I've already paid Jody a retainer. We're his clients now. He won't let that happen." Peter took her hand again. "You've told me a dark secret: I don't know that I can live the rest of my days with it hanging over us. Please, Jackie, this is what I need. As your husband. Do it for yourself, do it for me. For us."

Jackie closed her eyes and counted backwards from ten, with Peter holding her hand all the while. She opened her eyes.

"Yes, for us."

CHAPTER 26

"I don't recognize any of this," Jackie said as she and Peter drove down US-80 out of Montgomery. "Everything is different now. Even the airport. When I was a girl, that airport was a tiny little thing. Black folks weren't even allowed to work there, except as janitors."

"There's been a lot of years between 1962 and 2012, Jackie," replied Peter as he slid A Love Supreme into the CD player. "Now try to calm yourself a bit, we'll be there in thirty minutes, maybe less."

Jackie slid deeper into her seat and tried to relax some. This wasn't what she'd thought coming back would feel like. She'd expected familiar sites, familiar smells, and familiar places. Why do this, if the world she left behind didn't even exist anymore? Not a single building they passed looked the same, and the route was littered with new developments, some still under construction; it only added to her anxiety.

"Wait!" cried Jackie as they turned off the highway. "Is that Old Man Jack's? It is! Peter, it's still standing, that old place. When I was really young, we used to stop there on the way back from selling at the market. Mama would treat us to some penny candy if we'd sold well. It was our special secret, the three of us. She never told my daddy."

Peter laughed. He'd never seen a glint in his wife's eyes like he'd seen just now. The excitement of being home. It was the same feeling he got when he visited his own family back in Sacramento.

"You changed, just then, honey," Peter said. "In all these years, I've never seen a look on your face quite like that. Like you were twelve years old. You'll be glad we did this, I'm sure of it."

Jackie stiffened as they rounded the bend. "That's where the sheriff's should be, but that's not the same building. It looks newer."

"That's the address I got, they probably remodeled," replied Peter as he pulled up to the curb and parked. "Alright, honey, this is it. Jody knows what time our appointment is, he's just a phone call away. Remember, all he told them is that he has a client with some info about a cold case. That's all they know. The rest is up to us. Be brave."

Jackie looked up at her husband, and for once she hid nothing. Every ounce of love, every drop of penitence, and every bit of respect she had for him shone through. Peter returned her gaze, and although he didn't speak, he did understand. He wiped a tear from his cheek.

✖

After so many years away, Jackie had almost forgotten how polite people in Lowndes County really were. As they entered the station, the petite blonde receptionist had wished them a good morning, smiled widely, introduced herself, and chatted with them for a bit. Her name was Polly, and she'd instantly put Jackie at ease. By the time the sheriff came into the lobby and greeted them warmly, Jackie felt more confident than she had since the district principals' meeting.

Jackie had told her story, with Peter's help, as she once again revisited the horrors she'd left so far behind. She'd recounted every instance of rape she could remember. She'd told the sheriff that no father was listed on Tony's birth certificate, which was easy to corroborate by pulling up the birth records. She explained all about Linda, her disability, her innocence and bright heart, and finally her death. She'd admitted to killing Joe Lamar in self-defense. But above all else, she was emphatic about Peter's not knowing any of this until last week, when he'd immediately booked the tickets. She was determined that burden she might now bear would not touch her husband.

"Well I must say," began Sheriff Millhouse, "that we have been wondering on for you for some time, Ms. Russell."

"Macon, please, sheriff. I haven't been a Russell in a long time." In some ways, Jackie's old name felt strange to her, but she also wanted to reinforce how much she'd changed over the years.

"Very well," conceded the sheriff. "But I have to say, you're famous around here."

"Famous?" asked Jackie and Peter in unison.

"Yes, famous. We think of your case as bringing civil rights to this county."

Of all the things Jackie had anticipated the sheriff saying, she never could've imagined this. "I don't understand," she said, bewildered.

"It was your case that brought to light how badly domestic workers were treated in this town. How many of our women were being preyed on and abused by their employers. The hell they were living just to make ends meet. And once your story got out, black folks all around the county started rallying for change. When the laws changed in '65 and they couldn't stop us from voting anymore, we changed things around here. Elected our first black sheriff a couple years after. Now we're in all kinds of offices in this county. Jim Crow is nothing but a memory 'round here now."

Jackie smiled. Maybe she didn't recognize Lowndes County, but, certainly, that was for the better.

Peter jumped up. "Are you telling me, sir, that there's no charges on the books?"

"Not exactly," replied Sherriff Millhouse. "But it's long been assumed that Gloria—Jackie—was protecting herself from retribution when she ran. I don't see any reason to challenge that now. There's not a person in this county who wants to see her case reopened—I won't be the one to do it. We wouldn't have a real case anyhow; most of the evidence was destroyed when the old station flooded through in '86. I'm declining to take a formal statement."

Jackie began laughing. She couldn't help herself— the relief was too great. Knowing that all her suffering, all her years of secrets and cover-ups and hidden guilt, had sprung something new. Something good. Something she never could have planned. That Linda's death hadn't been for nothing. She jumped up and hugged Peter, overjoyed.

Sherriff Millhouse let the couple celebrate for a moment. "There is one loose end, ma'am, that I'd like for you to tie up. I think it's important." He reached over to his intercom. "Polly, send Deputy Green in here."

CHAPTER 27

"I don't know what loose ends he could be talking about," Jackie whispered, her voice tense. "With all I just told him, what more could there possibly be?"

Peter smiled encouragingly. "I'm sure it's just some small thing. Don't you worry, baby."

Sheriff Millhouse looked up from his paperwork as a knock came at the door. "That'll be Deputy Green now."

A young woman popped her head into the office. "You wanted to see me, Sheriff?"

"Come in. I'd like you to meet Mr. and Mrs. Macon. Mrs. Macon has some information that you and yours might be ... interested to know," replied the sheriff, a sly smile at his lips.

Jackie looked at the deputy, puzzled. The woman couldn't have yet been thirty years old, but there was something familiar in her face that Jackie couldn't put her finger on. In a daze, she exchanged pleasantries as the introductions continued.

"I expect, Deputy," the sheriff began, "that you know Mrs. Macon here by another name. This is Gloria Russell."

"Gloria Russell?" the young woman asked, confused. "I'm afraid I don't have any kin by… wait! Sherriff, are you telling me this is our Gloria Russell, my aunt?"

"Aunt?" exclaimed Jackie and Peter, almost simultaneously.

The Sherriff laughed. Deputy Green took Jackie by the hand, guided her to her feet, and looked her over with a broad smile on her face. Jackie returned the smile, stunned.

"You've come back!" exclaimed Deputy Green as she tackled Jackie in a bear hug. "All my life I've been hearing about you. Green is my married name—I'm your brother's daughter, Stephanie. I've got a whole heap of people waiting to meet you!"

⁂

Stephanie had called her father, then her husband, immediately. By the time twenty minutes had passed, her cell phone had blown up with text messages, and emails. It was all she could do to keep up with it all as she arranged a special dinner with her kin.

The reunion had been a joyful madness, but tinged with awkwardness in places. When Tony had arrived, Jackie had pounced on her son, now fifty years old, and taken him into her arms—almost like a baby—before Tony could get in so much as a word. Peter hung back, a bit overwhelmed, but nonetheless full of excitement.

Jackie and Peter had followed Stephanie in her squad car to what had once been the white part of town, but which now reflected faces of every shade. The family now sat, chatting excitedly, in the small function room of Russell's Grill & BBQ.

"Tell me, how did you come to own this place? It's a fine restaurant." Peter asked Michael. "I thought you said you were in construction?"

"I am," replied Michael. "But when Grandma B. passed, she left Tony and I three rental properties each. She'd started buying up land in the '70s, when most black folks were still a bit wary of crossing the river. Tony and I run this as a side business, rent out the others."

"Your Grandma," Jackie began, "I want you to know how good she was to me. Her reputation might've said otherwise, but she had just about the biggest heart I've ever known. She made a way for me when there was no way to be made. She saved my life, no question about that." Gloria turned to Tony. "I didn't want to leave you, baby, but I didn't have a choice. Black Gal promised she'd raise you as her own, and I never once had to doubt she'd hold true to her word."

"She did," answered Tony. "Her and Aunt Stella raised us as brothers. I was happy coming up, for the most part. But what I don't understand is why you didn't come back for me earlier. I spent a lot of my teenage years acting out, wondering why you never came for me— never even sent word. Not even after things changed. It haunted me. Don't know how I ever managed to marry my Yolanda—I did just about everything to push that woman away. Too scared of rejection, I guess, but she never quit on me."

"I never closed my heart to you," said Jackie. "Never. And not a day went by that I didn't think on you, pray on you. But the way I went, there was no coming back. It was Peter who convinced me to come now, and even still I was afraid of the Yellow Mama."

Peter chuckled, almost a laugh. "That chair was decommissioned years ago, Jackie. Even I knew that."

"I guess I … I still don't understand," continued Peter. "We turned ourselves into the most progressive town in Alabama a long time ago. With the Internet now… I just don't know."

"Come on, baby, let's you and me go set at the bar. Talk this through."

Tony nodded and the two excused themselves, leaving the others at the table. A hush fell over the group.

"Grandma B. passed some time ago," offered Stephanie to break the silence. "She probably wouldn't be thrilled with me joining the force, but more than anyone she was the one who encouraged me to be whatever I wanted to be. I'm the youngest female deputy this county has ever seen."

Michael laughed. "No, the law probably wouldn't have been her first choice, but she would've been proud of you all the same." He turned to Peter. "I don't know how much you know about my grandma, but…"

"Jackie's told me plenty," Peter chuckled. "Seems she wasn't opposed to bending a few rules here and there."

"Ain't that the truth," agreed Stephanie.

"But all that rule-bending left us well provided for," Michael went on. "I invested most of the money into my construction business. Didn't even lose too much when the markets crashed in '08. Now I'm on the upswing again— there's lots of new developments going up these days."

"I do hauling, myself," said Peter. "Got a small fleet, but it's growing. Been looking to expand outside of the state, too."

"There'd be plenty of work for you here. The government's practically throwing money at minority contractors now, and I haven't been able to find a reliable hauler yet."

Peter and Michael began discussing the industry. Stephanie chatted with one of the waitresses, who'd come to bring another round of sodas. She had no interest in construction; she'd already found her calling in life.

"Peter!" Jackie cried as she and Tony came back to the table. Both their faces were tear streaked but also reflected a peace that hadn't been there when they'd gotten up. "Watch how God works, we're grandparents! Tony's got two girls, Makayla and Lauren, both teenagers."

"That's wonderful Jackie, especially with us never having kids together. I hope we can meet the girls on our next trip." Peter replied excitedly.

"I know your Grandma Helen and even your Papa George would be proud of you, Tony," Jackie said as she sat down. "They must be smiling at you from above."

Tony and Michael looked at each other, surprised and unsure of what to say next.

"Jackie," Michael started slowly. "Papa George ain't gone from us yet. He's in a hospice home in the city. No one told you?"

"No," Jackie answered, "I had no idea. He must be well into his nineties now." Jackie didn't know how to name the feeling that had just dropped into her stomach—some mix of nostalgia, anger, and a prick of love—so she took Peter's hand to steady herself.

"After he … lost you and Linda," Tony explained, "he went bad. Real bad. Lost your old house inside of a couple years, I'm sorry to say. It was Grandma B. who got him help before he drank himself to death. He reformed after that. Became a deacon in the church and everything. Grandma B. never let him get too close to us, but she was the one who saved him just the same."

"You might consider going out to see him, Jackie," said Stephanie. "It won't be long now."

"Long now?" asked Jackie. She had a hundred other questions swirling in her mind already; this was the only one she managed to utter.

"Liver cancer," said Stephanie. "Last stages. Care workers say his body is starting to shut down now. A couple days at best."

"Jackie," said Peter, "it looks like you got one more challenge to meet before we leave town. But I got you, baby, I got you."

CHAPTER 28

I t was early in the day. Jackie had forgotten how the Alabama heat could rise with the sun, how the air itself could stick to her body as if it were a weight on her neck.

The hospice home wasn't far from the airport, only a few miles east. The drive from their hotel seemed to fly by, even though a fifty-year-old stone sunk heavily into Jackie's gut. Visiting hours began at 8:30 a.m., and—despite their jetlag—Jackie wanted to arrive first thing. Their flight wasn't until late in the afternoon, but Jackie knew how quickly "a couple of days," could turn into "I wish we had more time."

"Room 110," reported Peter as he returned from checking them in at the visitor's station. Jackie had held back in one of the waiting room's chairs; she wasn't up for pleasantries just now. "Seems he has a view of the back garden. The nurse said that's been some comfort to him."

Jackie didn't know how to respond. "Alright," she muttered.

"Jackie, you should know he'll be in and out," said

Peter gently. "Low-dose morphine drip. He was awake a few minutes ago, though. The aide managed to get him to take a few spoonfuls of breakfast."

"Alright," Jackie muttered again as she stood up. "Room 110, let's get to it." Peter reached for her hand, but she shrugged him off.

The room was dim, lit only by the sunlight streaming in from between the blinds and the glow of the morning news, on mute, coming from the TV. Monitors beeped, equipment hissed. An IV holder with far too many bags hung next to the bed, connected by a long snaking tube leading to George's wrist. Jackie gasped.

She looked down at the frail man now lying in the bed. He was much too thin, the lines in his skin were painfully sunken, and his closed and creased eyelids seemed made of tissue paper, but there was no mistaking her father's face.

"Daddy," she whispered timidly. "Daddy, it's me. It's Gloria."

George stirred weakly, but otherwise didn't respond. His eyes remained shut and unseeing.

"Daddy, it's Gloria. Your daughter. I've come back." Jackie waited a moment, hoping for a response.

"Peter, I can't," she whispered desperately. "I'm not even sure he knows I'm here."

"Keep going, baby. They say they can hear a lot," Peter soothed.

"Daddy, this is my husband, Peter. I brought him to meet you. We've been married now some twenty-five years. You always wanted me to find a good man, Daddy, remember?"

"Gloria?" came George's hoarse voice, barely a whisper. For a moment Jackie thought she'd imagined it. George coughed a painful, pitiful cough but then eked out, "You gone?"

"I came back Daddy, just yesterday. Michael and Tony told me where you were. I came as soon as visiting hours would permit."

Something very near a smile passed George's lips.

"I became a teacher after all, Daddy, and principal of my school these last eighteen years. I just retired last week."

"You should be proud of her, sir, all the students she's helped. Turned that school right around, too." Peter said.

George lifted his head slightly, acknowledging Peter for the first time. The effort was too much for him. He coughed again as he fell back into his pillow. He closed his eyes as he wheezed.

"I'm going to give you to a moment alone, Jackie," Peter said. "Take all the time you need; I'll be in the waiting room when you're ready."

Jackie nodded. She pulled a folding chair up to George's bed and took his hand.

"Daddy, you said I couldn't make it, but that was just the hardness of your life talking. I know you believed in me, like Mama. I know that in my heart now, Daddy. I've been thinking on it. You just wanted the world to be easier for me than it was for you. And when Mama left us, I never considered what that did to you. The guilt you must've borne."

The slightest squeeze of Jackie's hand, the weakest pressure, told her he understood. That Jackie's words were his truth.

Jackie sat by the bed for a long time, talking. Telling George all she'd done over the years. How Black Gal had sent her to Texas. About finishing high school in Denton, then moving onto college at the University of California. About the civil rights groups she'd joined, about the grassroots work she did in the '70s. About the curriculums she'd reformed in the '80s and '90s. About the students she'd helped in her classroom, no matter where they came from or the color of their skin. About the inclusion she strived for, and achieved, when she became principal. About how she ran her school as a place of fundamental respect, where all children could get a solid education. About meeting Peter, and how he supported her in everything she did.

Jackie didn't know how much her father heard, but she kept on talking until she'd run out of words. Until the stone in her stomach eroded away.

George started just after Jackie fell silent, as if he were afraid of the quiet. He visibly mustered his strength, then reached for her hand.

"I shoulda done better by you, Glowbug, but you turned out jus' fine all the same."

Jackie held her father's hand for a long, long moment before he drifted off. Whether to sleep or toward the gates to the next life, Jackie didn't want to know. She kissed her Daddy on the forehead and left the room silently.

EPILOGUE

"We should've done this years ago, Mama J.," said Tony. "I don't know why we never did. Richard did so much for this county."

"Well, it's righted now, that's all I can say. He was such a good man, Tony," replied Jackie as she lay the wreath on the memorial. She'd petitioned for a plaque in Richard's honor as soon as she and Peter had moved. But once the town got wind of it, the idea had blown up. Before Jackie knew it, the small plaque she'd envisioned turned into a full-blown ceremony, with the footbridge—which had been rebuilt only a few years earlier—being dedicated in Richard's name. Richard's widow and two children had come in from Montgomery, and his legal partner, now retired, had flown in from Tampa to speak. Even the local papers had come out for the dedication.

The crowds had gone now. Jackie had stayed at arm's length during the ceremony. This was a moment for Richard's family; no matter how much love had passed between the two of them those fifty-one years ago, she knew it wasn't her place to hold any claims. With Makayla's help, Jackie had started the petition anonymously online—seeing this day come to pass was enough for her.

"He helped me get you to safety at your Grandma B.'s all those years ago," said Jackie solemnly. "Did you know that?"

"He did?" exclaimed Tony. "I worked for him one summer, as an intern in Montgomery. He was a campaign manager then. He never told me."

"He couldn't tell you, baby," Jackie said softly. "But I'm glad you knew him some. He was a remarkable man."

"And what about me, huh?" Peter chided as he sauntered up and placed an arm around Jackie's shoulder.

"You're plenty remarkable, too, in your own way," laughed Jackie, before turning somber. "But Richard was my first love, Peter. That never goes away." Jackie shot a quick look at Tony, who got the message and wandered off.

"I know, baby. I'm just teasing you," replied Peter. "We were well past forty when we got married. We both have pasts, I know that."

"Yes, we do," agreed Jackie. "I used to think, Peter, that marrying you was just about the best thing I'd ever done, but I was wrong. This year's made me realize. The best thing is sharing my life, all of it, with you."